JILL AT HAZELMERE

JILL
AT
HAZELMERE

A STORY OF THE FOURTH FORM
AT HAZELMERE

by

VALERIE HASTINGS

THE CHILDREN'S PRESS
LONDON AND GLASGOW

This Impression 1965

CONTENTS

CHAP.		PAGE
1	SENDER UNKNOWN	11
2	THE NIGHT OF THE STORM	19
3	THE SECOND NOTE	27
4	UNEXPECTED DIFFICULTIES	34
5	TROUBLES INCREASE	41
6	NINA TURNS PRIVATE EYE	48
7	AN ACCIDENT	54
8	STRANGE BEHAVIOUR	65
9	IN THE ENEMY'S CAMP	73
10	A SHOCK	81
11	SURPRISING NEWS	89
12	CAUGHT!	98
13	WHO TOLD?	106
14	ABOUT LINDY	114
15	A CLUE AT LAST	125
16	SHOW-DOWN	137
17	TEA WITH MISS GEE	152

CHAPTER ONE

SENDER UNKNOWN

JILL RODGERS, newly elected captain of the fourth form at Hazelmere School, stared aghast at her close friend, Nina Cassel.

"Not go in to town? But it's our half-day and we're dolled up ready for the trip! I don't get it. Why?"

They were on their way downstairs and Nina had paused to peer over the banister rail. She pulled Jill to her side. "Look! A little way along the corridor is a box, hanging on the wall. Right?"

"Yes. But . . ."

"It's there for contributions to the fourth form magazine, in the shape of stories, gossip pars, poems, articles, etcetera. . . . No, don't explode, Jill. Just listen for a minute. Exactly opposite the box is the common-room door, and this very afternoon the room will be as vacant as it ever has been. Empty. Full of nothing but a blessed quiet, because it happens that *all* the girls are going out. That means we could work in peace. Positively no interruptions and no jabbering and giggles going on. Right, again?"

"So what?"

"I'm supposed to be editor and ought to be tackling the job. You, as captain of the form, simply must write a lively sports review for me—and it's your first one, Jill. It's got to be good. Don't forget Vilma Blake had nearly as many votes in the election as you, and her mob'll be eager to criticise. So let's give town a miss and get down to it. What do you say?"

Jill scowled, drew her mouth into a venomous pout and growled savagely. Then a hand passed over her face and her usual sunny expression was back. It was an odd little trick she always used when about to give way in an argument or undertake an unpleasant task. She said it helped her to get rid of resentment quickly. "You win, pal," she said now. "I'll go and collect writing things, while you look for treasures in the box. Good luck with the offerings."

"I'll need stacks of that. Don't think me too jaundiced if I say that in my opinion the fourth form isn't bursting at the seams with talent." Nina started to continue on her way down the stairs but turned as Jill said laughingly: "I bet several mistresses would agree whole-heartedly with that sentiment. You'd better start a talent crusade in your editorial columns. There's a remote possibility you might achieve something."

"Nobody—but nobody—reads editorials," Nina replied, turning away again. "Hurry, won't you?"

"I'll do that. See you in the common-room," Jill assured her, mounting the stairs two at a time.

In a few moments the girls were together again, in the unusually peaceful atmosphere of the common-room. Jill looked inquiringly at the three envelopes in Nina's hand. "All you've got?" she asked.

"Mmm. Can't think why I ever took this job on. I believe they really expect me to write the entire magazine myself. Good thing we only produce two issues a term. More would have me climbing up the wall."

"One of the penalties of wanting to make writing your career," Jill said unsympathetically. More seriously, she added: "And at least you haven't a constant feeling that someone's waiting to grab your place at the first opportunity."

"Too true," Nina agreed fervently. She knew just what was on Jill's mind; in fact she had reminded her friend of the situation only a few minutes ago. The form captain election had taken place because at the end of the previous term Pam Ralston had left the school suddenly to go abroad with her parents. Jill's victory over Vilma Blake had been by a very narrow margin and now, in these early days of the new term, there was still some strong support for Vilma. The odd misjudgment, a little bad luck, and Jill's leadership would certainly be challenged.

"Sorry, pal. I didn't mean to drag my troubles in," Jill apologised.

"Your troubles—my troubles. Same thing."

Jill impulsively squeezed Nina's hand. "You're a tower of strength—even though you're slim enough to be more like a spire than a tower."

They both giggled and Nina said: "Works both ways. Do me a really good sports article, one that'll stimulate them into violent enthusiasm. I'll stand you a cream tea as a reward. Now let's get stuck in. Drag a couple of chairs up to our usual table in the corner, while I open these so-called treasures. . . . Half a sec, though. No cream tea. You diet after holidays, don't you?"

"Not this term. All my spare cash went on discs, not eats. So what with that and the twist, I'm exactly what I weighed at the end of last term. Therefore I hold you to your offer."

"Okay. Cream tea. And I, unrewarded, will set about writing the rest of the mag." Nina's eyes, which had long dark lashes, narrowed as she laughed. "How about a page headed: 'In Memory Of Promised Contributions Which Failed To Arrive'?"

"Bit drastic. Try your three envelopes first. You may be lucky."

Nina had already opened the first envelope. It contained a poem. Definitely usable, she decided. The only trouble was that Helen wrote in the modern idiom and Miss Stubbins, the English mistress, would be certain to make acid comments about the fourth form magazine when it appeared. Where verse was concerned Miss Stubbins was inclined to be orthodox.

The second envelope was crumpled and ink-smeared. Nina held it up. "Creased and garnished like this it can only come from Judy." She took out a worn-looking sheet of paper speckled with blots. "She hasn't a clue as to what's meant by a gossip paragraph! All this will be stale news by to-morrow, never mind about when we get the issue run off on the Roneo."

"Even if any of it's true," Jill said. "You forget Judy's talent for inaccuracy."

"I'm reminded of it," Nina said grimly. "According to the second item I'm writing a play in my spare time."

"A play! That's rich, even for her."

"Wonderful, isn't it? Wait. I think I know how this started. I was talking to Lindy after the drama session and I did say something about if I couldn't write a better one-act play. . . . You know how one talks. Judy was passing at the time. I suppose she must have heard."

"And for the rest, two and two make five, six, or any number you fancy." Jill chuckled. "No great harm done. You put the editor's pencil through it."

"Resolving to have a few plain words with Judy. She's a menace. The things she dreams up!"

"One thing you have to grant," said Jill. "She's never spiteful. And she always believes she's got the story right."

"That's two things. And there'll be home truths from me just the same."

Jill grinned, knowing that Nina was really a very forgiving person.

Nina opened the third envelope. She stared at its contents and frowned.

"What is it?" Jill demanded.

"A little piece from somebody who doesn't give her name, and who writes in block letters. Read it yourself."

Jill took it from Nina. The neatly printed message was quite brief. It ran: A CERTAIN GIRL IN THE FOURTH FORM BREAKS SCHOOL RULES BY HAVING LIPSTICK IN HER POSSESSION AND USING IT WHEN SHE GOES TO TOWN ON HALF-DAYS.

The note referred to Lindy Sinclair; that was as obvious to Jill as it would be to anyone else in the Fourth. Something had changed Lindy. She'd always been a rather quiet, reserved girl, popular enough in her way. But she'd started the new term in a completely different mood, caring little or nothing for school activities and even less for studying. She made no secret of the fact that the sooner she could leave the better pleased she'd be, and she was acting as grown-up as she could.

Nina said: "Why go to the trouble of writing that? It's something we all know. If it's supposed to be a joke, well, how stupid can you get?"

Jill passed the paper back. "I wish we could simply forget it."

"Why not do just that?"

"Its being anonymous."

Nina nodded. "I see what you mean. Considered that way, it's rather poison-pen stuff, isn't it? Not serious, I know; but does it go on from here?"

"Your guess is as good as mine," said Jill. "But I have to confess my guess doesn't make me shout for joy."

There was a dead silence in the common-room as they looked at each other, their minds troubled.

On half-days the girls were permitted to collect tea trays from the kitchens and bring them to the common-room. Jill and Nina were having what they considered to be a well-earned break when the door was flung open and a short, rather plump girl rushed in.

"The end of our peaceful session," Jill said with resignation.

"Am I too late for tea?" the newcomer gasped. "Of all the rotten luck—when I was hurrying back I had to run into the Bish and she's booked me for dirty shoes!"

The Bish was one of the prefects, a girl named Beryl Bishop.

"Not to worry too much, Judy," said Nina. "You won't hear any more about it—unless you offend again. You should be more careful, though. You know the Bish has a thing about a neat appearance."

Judy Willets sighed. "I was so sure I'd cleaned them. I must have diverted myself." She looked at her watch. "I suppose I'm too late."

"There's plenty of tea here," Nina assured, "if you can find a cup."

"Thanks." Judy hesitated. "I'm afraid I'm a bit peckish."

Jill smiled. "How unusual! But you're in luck; we're well stocked with biscuits."

Judy drew up a chair. She wore thick glasses and these seemed to make her eyes big and wondering. As she sipped her tea she exclaimed: "Oh! I must tell you . . ."

"Half a mo," Nina interrupted. "If it's about the

play I'm supposed to be writing you can forget it. I'm not."

Judy looked astonished. "Is that true? But I felt certain I heard you say . . ." Her hand went to her mouth in dismay. "Oh, dear. And I made a tiny mention of it in my gossip contribution. . . ."

"Which is out," Nina said firmly.

"Out!" Judy's amazement was almost comic.

Nina went on: "To begin with, by the time the mag's issued the bits of gossip that are right will be stale news. And the bits that are wrong will be even more obviously wrong."

Judy shook her head sadly. "I so fancy working on a newspaper," she said plaintively, "and this is such good practice."

Jill laughed outright. "I'm sorry for any newspaper that gets landed with you, Judy. They'll spend half their time publishing apologies and corrections."

Nina added to this. "It's not much use being first with the news when it's false news, Judy."

"I must be more careful," Judy said contritely. She brightened up immediately. "But I was going to tell you. There's a new typist over in the offices. I suppose she's working for the bursar. She's ever so young. A teenager, I mean. I should think this must be her first job." She appealed to Nina. "How about that for a mag item?"

Nina shook her head. "School administration. That's out. We mind our own business."

"Her name's Ann Page. I suppose she's taken Miss Yates's place. Is it true Miss Yates left to get married?"

"Could be," Jill said.

Judy looked thoughtful. "I know someone else who'd like to leave—and I'm not talking about the staff."

"You wouldn't have Lindy in mind?" Nina suggested.

"How did you guess? I was going to have tea with her to-day—only I went to buy a Get Well card to send to my Aunt Dorothy. I was to meet Lindy afterwards." Judy hesitated in some confusion. "The truth is I'm broke. If Uncle Max forgets my birthday, I don't know what'll happen. Bankruptcy, I expect. So I was relying on Lindy. There was no sign of her, so I hung around for a while and then I saw her. She was in the new coffee bar and she'd forgotten about me. She was with three boys and I didn't like to gate-crash the party, so I caught the next bus back."

"Boys from St. Mark's?" Jill suggested.

"No, these were older." Judy was shaking her head vigorously. I saw some motor-bikes parked in the side alley. There were a couple of scooters, too. I reckon some of them belonged to the boys Lindy was with."

Judy was guessing, of course, but Jill felt worried. Boys from St. Mark's would have to be back at school in time for their call-over. It sounded as though the boys Lindy was probably with had left school, in which case they would be in no hurry and might well persuade her to stay out late. In her present mood she wouldn't need much coaxing.

Jill knew that Lindy had already stayed out late on one night this term and was very lucky not to be caught; but that sort of luck wouldn't last for ever. As captain of the form Jill felt she had a certain amount of responsibility. She would, she supposed, have to tackle Lindy. But would it do any good? She felt very doubtful. And the prospect was so uninviting that for the moment she wished her rival, Vilma Blake, had won the captaincy election. Anyone—just anyone but me, she thought.

CHAPTER TWO

THE NIGHT OF THE STORM

LINDY SINCLAIR approached the school gates warily. The bold recklessness she had felt in town was fast evaporating, indeed had almost gone. She had found it so easy to tell the boys she couldn't care less about breaking rules by returning late; but now that she was doing it she was scared and fluttery. She was very wet, too, because one of the boys had given her a lift on his scooter and the rain had started suddenly. It was falling heavily now and the strengthening wind was driving it hard.

The weather offered one advantage, though. No prefect would be on gate duty, which was a surprise check made sometimes.

As Lindy expected, the main gates were locked; but there was a small one at the side which was still open. Once in the grounds she kept to the bushes and scurried round to the back of the main school building.

With her hat and raincoat left to dry in a corner of the cloakroom she felt safer. But there was still the common room to be reached and the risk of encountering Beryl Bishop or one of the other prefects. Lindy decided to chance the back stairs, which meant passing a corridor leading to matron's quarters. Her luck held, and a minute or two later she was stepping into the common-room, trying to look as though she'd been around all evening.

In this she wasn't so successful. Jill, who was near the door, gave her a startled glance and exclaimed: "Lindy, you're soaked!"

Lindy looked down in consternation. She hadn't realised just how much damage the rain had done. She appealed quickly: "Don't give me away, Jill."

"Nip up to the dorm and change. Otherwise you'll be running a temp. and then there'll surely be questions," Jill said at once.

It was a dismaying prospect. Lindy turned and fled. Jill closed the door after her, wondering how many girls had noticed Lindy's wet clothes. One certainly had. This was Vilma Blake, who came close to Jill and said sharply: "I can see all of us losing privileges, thanks to that girl."

Vilma's outstanding fault was her quick, fiery temper; but this time Jill felt some sympathy. She said quietly: "Yes, I'm worried." She was a little on her guard, too, for it was never easy to guess what was going on under Vilma's chestnut coloured hair. Her eyes, greenish in certain lights, didn't give much away, either.

There was an awkward silence. Then Vilma said: "I'm not trying to interfere—but someone should talk to her, you know."

She left unsaid that it was Jill's reponsibility; but Jill realised this. She sighed. "I'm game to try, only I can't see it doing much good. Still, it's up to me."

Vilma nodded and started to move away, but Jill called her back. Anxious to get election rivalries buried, and to avoid the Fourth being split into two factions, Jill had just made a difficult decision. She felt that the sooner she mentioned it, the better.

"The tennis tournaments," she said.

Vilma raised her eyebrows. "You've picked the team?"

Jill shook her head. "I'm hoping you'll do that. If I put up a note to say you've accepted the tennis captaincy, then the rest will be up to you."

There was only a slight hesitation before Vilma exclaimed: "Jill, that's pretty decent of you! After all, as form captain you're fully entitled to take over the tennis yourself—and I know you're dead keen."

Jill smiled, pleased by the tribute. "Keenness isn't everything. For one thing, I'm not the form's best player."

"You're a jolly useful one," Vilma said. "You can cope with a powerful serve and give as good as you get— which is something very necessary when we meet St. Hilda's Fourth." She paused, then went on briskly: "Okay. Thanks. You're in the team, of course, and I'd like Nina, too."

This surprised Jill. "Really? She's no power player."

"But so light on her feet she's across the court before you realise what goes on. At least two of the St. Hilda's team will seem like pounding hippos up against a gazelle."

Jill laughed. "Do hippos pound? It's a wonderful thought. But seriously, Vilma, I know Nina will be delighted. She doesn't fancy her chances for the team. Who's your fourth?"

Vilma grimaced. "We've been talking about her."

"Oh, Lindy." Jill shook her head. "When she's on form, yes. But can you rely on her? Right now her chief interest seems to be in showing *no* interest."

"Which brings us back to your heart to heart with her, doesn't it?"

Jill sighed. "I suppose so."

She slipped quietly away and hurried up to the dormitory. It was already dark but only one of the bedside lamps was burning. Lindy had changed her clothes and was at a window, peering out. She turned as Jill entered.

"Just listen to the wind. It's dreadful now. Unless it drops I can't imagine anyone being able to sleep."

"Certainly not with this next window rattling away." Jill went to it, found a piece of paper in the pocket of her cardigan, and proceeded to plug the window. "There— that should do it."

Lindy said: "I don't think there's so much rain now; just the wind. I've never heard it so loud. Like a hurricane. Not that I've ever been through one, but I've had it described to me."

"I should think it's much worse than this. Some of the news films make hurricanes look absolutely frightful."

"But exciting!" Lindy exclaimed.

Jill nodded her head slowly. Then she joined Lindy at her window and said: "You find life pretty dull, don't you?"

"That's an understatement." Lindy wasn't looking at her.

Jill said: "What *do* you want?"

Lindy still stared out, though there was little she could see. "Anything, so long as it's different. . . . And miles away from school."

"Haven't you ever enjoyed being at Hazelmere?"

"Oh, yes. But I'm bored with the place now."

"You'll have to snap out of it, Lindy," Jill said. "Being bored only leads to being more bored."

Lindy shrugged her shoulders. "I'm not expecting magic." Suddenly she gave a little gasp of alarm and clutched Jill's arm. "What was that? You must have heard it!"

"Something blew down. At a guess I'd say some fencing."

"Should we go out and see?"

Jill hesitated. "Not too wise. If we're seen we'll only be sent back." She squeezed Lindy's arm momentarily. "Besides, if odd pieces of wood and tiles are blowing about I prefer to stay under cover. Of course, if you don't mind collecting a cracked head. . . ."

Lindy turned away. "The whole place can blow down so far as I'm concerned," she said, sounding so surly that Jill decided to postpone the serious talk. Right now it would be a sheer waste of breath.

It was, of course, Judy who was first with the news. She came in last for breakfast, which was extraordinary, and as she took her place next to Nina she said, wide-eyed and eager: "Have you heard?"

"Heard what?" Nina asked.

"There was a terrible storm last night. . . ."

"Forgive me for not registering surprise. As it kept me awake most of the night. . . ."

"Me, too," said Vilma, who was sitting opposite. "I thought the roof was coming off."

"Not the roof—apart from two or three tiles," Judy said. She paused for effect, made sure the others were listening, then dropped the bombshell. "But the sports pavilion—it's a wreck!"

"Oh, no!" Jill exclaimed. "Not the pavilion!"

"It is," Judy maintained. "And I'm not making it up. Honestly, I'm not. Old Mangold-wurzel told me." She was referring to the gardener who was popularly known by this name.

Ruth Tranter, one of the girls on the other side of the table, laughed. "I bet he was pulling your leg. He knows you swallow stories like a whale swallows—er— what does a whale swallow?"

"Jonahs," Nina suggested.

"Biology class. Plankton," Jill said. "Swimming organisms found . . ."

Judy almost beat her fists on the table in exasperation.

"It's perfectly true. Old Mangold-wurzel was no end upset."

Nina looked at Jill. "There may actually have been some damage," she said quietly. "After all, bits of it are shaky, we know, and need repairs."

Jill glanced at her watch. "Between breakfast and first lesson there's just about time to nip down to Long Field and check."

Ruth was saying: "Judy, remember the time you told old Mangold-wurzel his cottage was on fire, when it was only some rubbish being burnt in the next field?"

"Why bring that up?" Judy sounded aggrieved.

"Could be his own back," Ruth said.

"Nothing of the sort!" Judy exclaimed.

"Quiet!" Jill hissed. "The Bish is looking this way. Do you want to get booked for being noisy at table?"

Judy was instantly subdued, but under her breath she said: "I tell you it's a wreck. You'll find out."

Which was what Jill and Nina did at the first opportunity. Before they reached Long Field they could see there was plenty of truth in Judy's story. When they came nearer and saw the full extent of the havoc it brought gloomy expressions to both their faces.

Most of the roof had gone. The large windows in the front were broken and the white frontage of the veranda was leaning outwards at such an angle it seemed likely to fall flat at any minute. One end of the pavilion had been battered out, while all the inside partitions were down and splintered. For yards around the field was littered with debris.

"What a mess!" Nina groaned. "It looks to me as though that's the finish of the old pavilion. Easier to built a new one than to repair all this lot, I should think."

Jill was too stunned to say more than: "I'm sure you're right."

The girls walked back to the school in almost complete silence.

There was no other serious damage done to school property by the freak storm. Some nearby riding stables had suffered, but without harm to any of the horses. So the wrecked sports pavilion became the talking point of the day and provided a challenge to Jill in the evening. It was Ruth Tranter who delivered it, shortly after prep. "What's going to be done about the pavilion, Jill?" she asked.

"I don't know," Jill said. "I haven't heard anything official so far. Have you?"

Ruth shook her head. "But you're in the best position to find out."

"How come?"

"There's a sports committee for the entire school. And the captain of the Fourth is a member. Simple as that."

"Help! I'd quite forgotten! Well—no emergency meeting has been called, unless the others have forgotten *me*."

Ruth hesitated. "There'll have to be a meeting, surely?"

"I imagine so."

Nina had joined them in time to hear Ruth's last comment. She said: "There's sure to be. I suppose Miss Frant will call it. After all, she's games mistress and chairman—or is it chairwoman—of the committee."

Ruth still gave all her attention to Jill. "Do you remember that there was a lot of talk last term about an extension to the pavilion?"

Jill nodded.

"I know Pam Ralston put the suggestion forward," Ruth went on. "I suppose now she's left the whole thing's been dropped."

"This seems the right time to bring it up again," Jill replied without hesitation.

"The form'll be glad to hear that. They're all saying that if the pavilion's repaired there must be an extension. Of course, better still—a new and larger one."

Having said this, Ruth hurried away. Nina turned anxiously to Jill. "Bearing in mind that Ruth's the leading light of the ' Vilma-Blake-for-captain ' movement, that sounds extraordinarily like an ultimatum to me. You know—' If you want to survive as captain get us more pavilion.' I'm sure that's what they're saying."

"But what can I do?" Jill protested. "Nothing more than put up the idea."

"*And* be very persuasive," Nina reminded.

Jill thought of that brief and disappointing talk with Lindy on the previous night. She bit her lip in annoyance at her own shortcomings. "I wish I'd a talent for it," she said glumly.

Nina laughed. "Cheer up! If you had, you'd probably end up selling vacuum-cleaners; and that would shock your father."

Jill had to smile. "Poor dear. I've already shaken him more than a bit, by wanting to be a vet instead of a doctor!"

CHAPTER THREE

THE SECOND NOTE

IT was two days since the pavilion had been wrecked by the violent storm. Jill, changed for tennis, was waiting for Nina and thinking rather nervously of the sports committee meeting which had been called for that evening. The main topic for discussion was to be the pavilion and Jill had been left in no doubt that the entire fourth form expected a lot from her. At an impromptu gathering in the common-room when they had all bombarded her, she had pointed out that the representatives of the fifth and sixth forms would doubt-less be equally keen on a brand new pavilion but they would not be so concerned about its size. It was only the fourth form, larger than the other two, which had felt so overcrowded. "I'm the newest and most junior member," Jill had explained, "and they're not going to take an awful lot of notice of me. That's only natural."

"So it's all the more up to you to make yourself felt and insist on the rights of our form to consideration," called one of Vilma's supporters.

"I'm not suggesting I won't do my best," Jill had replied rather heatedly. "But you've got to under-stand . . ."

There was a chorus of: "Bigger and better, Jill. That's what we want."

Of all people, it was Vilma Blake who told them to shut up and give Jill a hearing, and Jill, remembering it now with appreciation, thought it a generous gesture which had probably prevented a nasty wrangle between her own supporters and Vilma's. I didn't come out of it too well, she decided. I'll have to learn to control a meeting better than that. All the same, I'll be out on a limb. One mistress, four girls from the Sixth—three of them prefects—and a girl from the Fifth. If they don't like my suggestion, and I can't be persuasive enough, what the heck's left for me to try?

It was impossible to answer this question, but she was still pondering it gloomily when Nina joined her. And Nina wasn't looking too happy, either. Jill took one look at her and said: "*Now* what's wrong?"

"The magazine, Jill. You know I put up a notice asking for stuff because we haven't nearly enough for this next issue?"

Jill nodded. "No response?"

"Worse than that—the wrong kind. I looked in the box on my way down here and found this." She took an envelope from her blazer pocket and handed it to Jill. The envelope was addressed in block letters to the editor. Inside was a solitary sheet of paper and the writing on it was also in block letters. Jill read aloud: "A FOURTH FORM GIRL WAS LATE GETTING BACK FROM TOWN ON WEDNESDAY. AND WAS SHE WET! ONE OF THESE DAYS SHE'LL BE CAUGHT."

Jill folded the paper and slipped it back into the envelope. "Just like the last one," she said.

The two girls exchanged troubled glances. Nina broke the silence. "I don't think we can write it off as a joke."

"I'm sure of that," Jill said. She frowned. "The first note was about Lindy, too. Does it mean someone's trying to warn her—or get us to warn her? Or does someone *want* her to be in trouble?"

"That's what I think. We've something sneaky here,

Jill. But how do we find out who sent it? The position of the mag box isn't going to help. Out in a corridor practically everyone uses. It's like the High Street sometimes."

"So that leaves us with the question—how many people knew about Lindy coming in late, soaked to the skin?" Jill concentrated. "I did, of course. So did Vilma Blake." Nina grimaced and shook her head. "Vilma's far from being my favourite person, but she wouldn't stoop to this sort of thing. If Lindy annoyed her in any way she'd go for her. You know Vilma's flaring temper."

Jill agreed. "There's Judy, I suppose. She was in town with Lindy and knew what was going on, and she was fairly near the door when Lindy looked in. But I can't think. . . ."

Nina was emphatic. "Judy's an empty-headed little gossip. No sense of discretion. But she's never been malicious." She took the envelope from Jill. "This isn't in her line at all."

"Then who?" Jill asked. "There were several people around when I persuaded Lindy to go up to the dorm and change. I can't remember names."

"Most of us were in the common-room," Nina said. "I didn't notice Lindy, because I was reading; but I suppose almost any member of the form might have seen her and realised she'd only just come in. But who in the form would do this sort of thing?"

Jill shook her head. "I'm not trying to make out we're wonderful; but there are limits and I just can't see any of our lot as a poison-pen expert."

"But would anyone in another form be sufficiently interested?" Nina suggested.

"I'd say not. And that gets us—where?"

"Nowhere. We have to wait for the next, if there's

going to be another. Honestly, I'm scared of unlocking the box."

"Don't show it," Jill cautioned. "After all, the mystery writer must know you've received the two notes. She'll surely be watching to see how you react."

"Which is an idea I don't like one little bit." Nina took up the racket she'd laid aside. "Come on, let's play."

Towards the end of the set quite a number of girls gathered round the court on which Nina and Jill were playing. Among them was Vilma Blake, who took Jill on one side afterwards and said: "You see what I mean about Nina? If you'd been a bit slower . . ."

Jill, still a little breathless, nodded. "I do see. She had me running all over the court. How did you get on?"

Vilma scowled. "Not well. Lindy didn't turn up. Can't do anything about that; it's not a compulsory. I tried out one or two possibles. Ruth Tranter . . ." She shook her head.

" Don't think I've ever played her," said Jill.

"Forehand too weak. Even with bags of training I don't see her making the grade." Vilma brushed some strands of hair from her forehead impatiently. "I suppose Denise is as good as anyone."

"I've played her. It was a doubles match and she partnered Lindy, who overshadowed her."

"Lindy on form is the one we need," Vilma said. There was a hint of challenge in her tone. "I can select her for the team, but I can't guarantee she won't immediately retort with a resignation from it. Or that if she does agree she'll pull her weight. Candidly, if we're to win we'll have to train hard and how do we get Lindy settling down to that?"

Jill didn't know; but she wasn't going to evade her responsibilibites. "I'll tackle her," she promised.

Vilma nodded, then hesitated. "I do think it's up to you, as captain. All the same, if you want me to . . ."

"I'll see it through," Jill said quickly, eager to avert even the appearance of an argument with Vilma about this. Too many people would delight in trying to make capital of it. Nina had already towelled and was walking slowly back towards the school buildings. Jill had just overtaken her when a breathless Judy joined them.

"I've just heard something—something odd!" Judy gasped.

Nina smiled quizzically. "Perhaps it seems odd because you didn't get it right," she suggested.

Judy looked offended. "Nina! Just because I made a slight mistake about you and writing a play!" she protested.

"A *slight* mistake—that's a gigantic understatement!"

"I did apologise, didn't I?"

"No harm done," Nina said. "Only you never learn. You keep on producing wild stories."

"I was right about the pavilion, and old Mangold-wurzel told me this one, too. He's only just told me. His brother works—or did work—for Colonel Ashcroft. Only the colonel's started to do some very strange things."

Jill, looking sternly at Judy, said sharply: "Be careful what you're saying, Judy. The colonel's been very good to the school."

"Too true," Nina emphasised. "We're free to wander in the woods on his estate. We can cross his fields—and I believe he rents one of them to us very cheaply. He's always turned up trumps on sports day."

"He's a perfect pet," Jill said. "I'm not going to hear anything bad about him, Judy."

"It isn't bad—not exactly." Judy looked troubled.
"I wouldn't say nasty things about him. But—well, he's
getting a bit old, isn't he? His hair's white. And old
people do turn eccentric. I don't suppose there's anything
more to it than that. But . . ."

"As you've not said what, I haven't a clue."

"You told me not to tell!" Judy protested, with some
justification.

Jill hesitated. She was quite prepared to send Judy off
with her tale untold. But how long would the chatterbox
keep it to herself? And if it was absurd or very unlikely
there was a chance of pointing this out to Judy before
any damage was done. So she nodded. "Very well,
you may tell us, Judy. But be sure you don't exaggerate
any of it."

"I'll tell it just as I was told." Judy promised. "The
colonel is sacking everybody. All his servants, including
old Mangold-wurzel's brother. There! That's very
strange, you have to admit."

"Perhaps so," Jill agreed, slowly. "But it really isn't
any concern of ours. Who he employs, or doesn't employ,
is his own business."

Judy nodded. "Yes, I can see that. But I still think it's
very odd."

"It seems odd, yes. But we don't know his reasons
and it's still nothing to do with us." Jill added emphatically: "I'm sure you shouldn't spread that story, Judy."

"Okay," Judy said. "I'll be discreet." She looked
resentfully at Nina, who'd whistled softly. "I can keep
quiet about things—I'll show you." She suddenly became
thoughtful. "I say, thinking about the colonel and his
white hair—I wonder how I'd look with white hair.
You know, *bouffante*."

"Oh, no!" Jill gasped.

"It's all very well for you and Nina. You're sungold blonde and Nina's raven black; neither of you have to see a pale uninteresting brown every time you look in a mirror! I'll have to do something about it one of these days."

"Don't rush into it," Nina advised. "Take your time. It's a very serious matter changing your appearance. If you go for the wrong style you'll come out looking a mess."

"Crikey! I hadn't thought of that. Yes, I'll be careful. Thanks for warning me. I'll borrow some magazines and look through with real concentration."

Judy hurried off purposefully. Jill exclaimed: "Good for you, Nina. All thought of Colonel Ashcroft's strange behaviour's been swept from her addled pate. And she's not likely to do anything drastic about her hair—not until she's able to get in to town. Anything could happen then."

Nina laughed. "Don't add that to your worries, Jill. I can cope with Judy. I'll keep her hovering on the edge of a decision. You know, this tint or that. Get her in a real dither and she'll end up doing nothing."

"Okay—provided she comes to you for advice." Jill frowned. "Oddly enough, we didn't see much of her during free time yesterday afternoon. Normally, there's no getting rid of her. I wonder where she went."

"Don't!" Nina pleaded. "Last thing we want is another version of Lindy-trouble. If that happens—I give up!"

CHAPTER FOUR

UNEXPECTED DIFFICULTIES

"Best of luck," Nina whispered, giving Jill an encouraging pat.

"You can say that again," Jill replied with a wry smile. She wasn't looking forward with any sort of pleasure to the meeting of the sports committee, not with the fourth form expecting so much from her.

Nina guessed what was bothering her and said: "I'm pretty sure you won't be entirely out on your own when you suggest the pavilion extension. I reckon Miss Frant'll be sympathetic. Then don't forget the Bish is generally fair-minded and might support you. Could be your day."

"I doubt it," Jill murmured as she hurried off.

The meeting was being held in the school library. This was in the oldest part of the building, and Jill loved the room for its mullioned windows and wonderful oak panels. There was usually an atmosphere of restful quiet, but that wasn't true of it now. The sixth form girls were already sitting at the big refectory table and there seemed to be some disagreement, but this was quickly suppressed when Jill joined them. She was followed by Mary Curtis, a tall girl who might easily be mistaken for a sixth-former, though she was actually head girl of the fifth form.

She winked at Jill and murmured: "Trouble among our betters. Hilda Wighton and the Bish, I'll wager. They're always at outs."

The clock gave its mellow chime and Miss Frant came hurrying into the library, taking her place at the head of the table. She was one of the youngest of the Hazelmere mistresses and had an impressive record in amateur sports, particularly for swimming and tennis. Her popularity was not based only on her achievements; she had a direct manner which appealed to the girls because they knew exactly where they were with her. Typically, she came straight to the point now.

"You all know why I've called this meeting. It's so that we can put our heads together and find the best way to cope with the wretched business of the wrecked pavilion." And she went on to explain that repairs would cost a lot and that the sports fund was not in a very healthy state.

"After essential repairs," Miss Frant summed up, "we're going to have to economise for the next term or two."

There was a gloomy silence.

Miss Frant added: "Unfortunately, there'll be no help from insurance on the pavilion. We were covered for fire, malicious damage, and so on; but there was no coverage for natural catastrophes such as storm and flood."

Jill's heart seemed to shrink right down to her shoes. Miss Frant was only talking of essential repairs. If even these meant future economy in sports affairs how could she possibly demand a larger pavilion?

But there was worse to come. Before the girls had recovered from the shock of the financial situation Miss Frant announced: "There is, I'm afraid, a further complication. The damaged pavilion stands in Long Field and I expect you know that we rent the field from Colonel Ashcroft. There's never been a legal agreement, but it's always been understood that he would eventually make a gift of the land to the school. That's one of the reasons why the building was erected in Long Field."

A thought flashed into Jill's mind. The colonel's strange behaviour—perhaps it wasn't one of Judy's wild stories. Perhaps it was true. Had the colonel changed and suddenly become difficult with everybody?

Miss Frant continued: "Well, we've rather been counting our chickens. Not only is it unlikely that the field will ever be given to the school, but it's very doubtful whether we can continue to rent it."

There was a gasp of dismay. The loss of Long Field, which was the largest of the sports fields and used for hockey and archery, would be an awful blow.

Beryl Bishop exclaimed: "I just don't understand! The colonel's always been so friendly and helpful."

"It's not his fault, poor man," Miss Frant said. "He's most unhappy about the whole thing. There's a family business and it's in serious trouble. He's selling up to save the situation. The house, estate, everything."

Jill was immediately sorry for the colonel and she felt her personal regrets were rather selfish; but it was a horribly gloomy thought that there'd be no more picnics and rambles in the woods. And they'd always been free to ride across his fields, too. . . .

Mary Curtis said: "Poor Colonel Ashcroft. Poor us, as well. It's going to make a gigantic difference."

"I'm afraid so," Miss Frant said. "And you can see, of course, how it makes the pavilion problem worse. It's not just repair work; it'll have to be moved, which will cost more money."

The Bish said suddenly: "What about the new owner, Miss Frant. Is there any chance of the field letting being continued?"

"I understand a Miss Garfield is buying the estate. So far, Colonel Ashcroft has not met the lady, everything is being done through her solicitors. But he'll be seeing her and he offered to plead our cause."

"So it could work out right!" one of the sixth form girls exclaimed.

Miss Frant thought it would be a mistake to be very optimistic. This was unnecessary advice so far as Jill was concerned. She felt absolutely gloomy. Clearly, if all the spare money was going on moving the pavilion to a new site and then carrying out essential repairs, there wasn't the slightest hope of any enlargemennt or improvements. Unless . . .

"We could try raising funds—that's the only way."

Everyone looked inquiringly at Jill, who felt horribly embarrassed. It was sheer bad luck that she should unconsciously think aloud at the very moment when all the others had stopped talking! If she could have been granted one wish it would have been for the floor to open and let her sink right out of sight.

Miss Frant said: "We can manage the pavilion repair without making any appeals, Jill. That's what you have in mind, I suppose?"

Jill hesitated, conscious that everyone was gazing at her. Mary Curtis said encouragingly: "If you've got a bright idea—share it."

Jill took the plunge, rather desperately. "What I was thinking, Miss Frant, is that if we have to more or less rebuild the pavilion it seems such a pity that it can't be improved at the same time. It *is* a bit on the small side and . . ."

Hilda Wighton said sharply: "Nonsense. It's quite satisfactory as it is."

"That suggestion has been put forward in the past,"

Beryl Bishop remarked placidly. "It was considered worthy of—further consideration." She smiled.

Mary Curtis, who was sitting opposite Jill, leaned forward and said in an undertone: "Now watch the fur fly."

Jill didn't understand, but while she was trying to work it out, Hilda Wighton said: "It's obviously a waste of time now, with funds being so low."

"But Jill's point was concerned with *raising* money," the Bish commented. She was smooth and unruffled.

Miss Frant intervened. "I don't think we can appeal to the school governors and such people. Everything seems to be costing more and we've gone to them quite a lot recently."

"I—I wondered about a concert," Jill said.

The words were hardly out of her mouth before Hilda Wighton was snapping: "Too much work with no guarantee of success." And at the same time the Bish was declaring: "Now that's quite an idea."

The two sixth-formers looked at each other challengingly. There were slightly flushed patches on Hilda Wighton's normally pale cheeks. Beryl Bishop still looked amiable.

Miss Frant said: "There are clearly two opposing points of view. I think we must vote. Jill Rodgers proposed a concert to raise funds for improving the pavilion at the time of repairs to it. Who seconds?"

"I do," Beryl Bishop said firmly.

"Those in favour," Miss Frant said.

Jill waited breathlessly. She started to count the raised hands. Beryl Bishop. Mary Curtis. A prefect named Mona Galton. This only left Hilda Wighton and one other sixth-former, who slowly raised her hand.

"It seems to be carried," Miss Frant commented.

Mary Curtis leaned across the table. "Congrats, Jill—but have you let us in for a packet of work!"

"I'm just beginning to realise that," Jill said. "Gosh! How I wish I wasn't here!"

When the meeting was over Jill was still feeling bewildered by the acceptance of her suggestion, and more than a little scared at the prospect of all the work involved.

"I wish I'd kept my big mouth shut," she confided to Mary Curtis. "Having proposed a concert I'll have to more than pull my weight—and that goes for the entire form, too. Wonder how they'll take it."

"With enthusiasm, I guess. Not to worry, Jill."

"Can't help it. Phew! I almost wish the Bish hadn't backed me up."

Mary Curtis winked. "That was largely because Hilda Wighton said ' No.' The gossip about our betters is that those two are known as the Natural Opposites. If one says ' yes ' the other says ' no '—just as a matter of course. Well, it's helped you."

"Has it?" Jill said very doubtfully. And in this far from happy frame of mind she reached the common-room. As she feared, it was crowded and the instant she opened the door questions were fired at her.

"Give me a chance!" she shouted.

At last there was an uneasy silence which threatened to break into noisy disorder any moment. A chair was pushed forward for Jill to stand on, but she rejected it. "I'm no soap-box orator," she said. "In fact I don't feel like any kind of orator."

"We want news, not—not orations," Ruth Tranter said.

Vilma Blake said: "Suppose you let Jill do the talking, then you'll get it." The completely unexpected rebuke had the effect of reducing Ruth to an injured silence.

"There's plenty of news," Jill said. "Most of it bad, I'm afraid. Let's get the worst over."

There were murmurs of disappointment as Jill told them about Colonel Ashcroft selling up. And the dismay increased as the girls realised just how much difference all this would make to them.

Judy cried despairingly: "But what about the woods? Are they going to be closed to us?"

"Nobody knows yet," said Jill. "It's going to depend on what Miss Garfield's like."

"An ogre, I'll bet anything," Muriel asserted. She was the form's pessimist.

Nina said: "No woods, no fields to ride across—and all this in addition to losing Long Field. Jill! Didn't anything good happen? Not anything at all?"

"Coming to that now," Jill said. To her great relief the proposal of a concert to raise funds for a better pavilion was greeted with immense enthusiasm. Even the most ardent supporters of Vilma Blake, such as Ruth, were completely in favour. In fact, there was only one member of the fourth form who was against the whole idea. This was Lindy Sinclair.

There was a general and extremely lively discussion about the Fourth's contribution to the concert and Jill took advantage of this to go across to where Lindy was standing.

"Lindy," she said. "You're far and away our best pop singer. You'll do a couple of numbers, won't you?"

Lindy, who was already looking sulky, scowled. "Sorry, Jill. I've no interest whatever in this silly old concert. You can leave me right outside." And before Jill could say a word, Lindy swung round and darted from the room.

"What's eating her?" Nina, at Jill's shoulder, demanded.

Jill sighed. "I just haven't a clue." Lowering her voice she said: "I'm sure Lindy's needing help of some kind—but what's the use? She throws everything back in your face."

CHAPTER FIVE

TROUBLES INCREASE

PLANS FOR their contribution to the concert occupied the spare time of most fourth formers for the next few days. Jill said to Nina: "Poor concert committee! Our lot already have enough suggestions to fill a three-day festival."

They were returning from the model kitchen after a domestic science period spent in making small cakes. Judy overtook them and cried: "I've had a wizard idea! Came to me while I was stirring the cake mixture."

Jill and Nina groaned.

"Don't be beastly! I'm thinking of more money for the pavilion fund. Suppose we run refreshments at the concert—and do the sandwiches and cakes. . . ."

"Help!" Jill exclaimed, throwing up her hands in horror.

"Remembering what your batch of cakes looked like . . ." Nina said thoughtfully.

"The timing went a bit wrong," Judy said. "But if I concentrated hard. . . ."

"Nobody's going to let us use the kitchen—or provide us with the necessary raw materials," Jill explained. "And have you thought about the cleaning up afterwards?"

Judy looked at her blankly. "Oh! I see what you mean. Perhaps it'd be better to forget all about it."

Jill winked at Nina. "I believe the Fifth are having something to do with the refreshments; serving and so on. They'll probably welcome a bit of extra help on the night. Why not have a word with Mary Curtis?"

Judy said hastily: "No. I'd rather forget the whole thing. After all, too many cooks." She hurried away.

Nina gurgled with laughter. "Too many cooks! It only needs one like Judy!"

They entered the school building and made their way up the stairs. Nina said: "Only one more period, thank goodness. I've had enough study for one day."

"As it's English Lit. we might manage to divert the lesson via drama to the concert," Jill suggested.

Miss Stubbins had a cold and the lesson was to be taken by Miss Latimer, who was their form mistress. Nina said: "I'm not so sure. The Latimer may prove to be very kind and understanding; but the exterior's a trifle chilly. She might not appreciate diversions."

"You could be right. We'll play it safe," Jill said, reminded that as this was Miss Latimer's first term she was still something of an unknown quantity.

They were near the common room and Nina paused at the magazine box. "I'm getting a thing about this—dreading what may be inside."

"Might as well look," Jill suggested.

Nina searched for the key and even then held back. "It's having a hypnotic effect, Jill. One time I could go past this box no end of times without even seeing it. Now it's the only thing I do see. I almost tiptoe past it."

"Open it—go on," Jill commanded.

"Okay." Nina obeyed. She produced a solitary envelope and without giving it more than a casual glance handed it to Jill. "I don't want to look. I've got a feeling."

Jill recognised the block letters on the envelope and there was an unpleasant chill sensation down her spine. She was tempted to crumple the envelope into her pocket and then burn it at the first opportunity—unopened. But Nina, who'd closed and locked the box, was gazing at her.

"It is, Jill, isn't it?"

Jill nodded her head slowly. Then she came to a decision. "Let's nip along to the library. We don't want to be caught by any of the others; I'm sure we look like conspirators."

Nina glanced at her watch. "Right. We've five minutes before Eng. Lit."

They hurried to the library, entering it very quietly and, for the benefit of a prefect who was sitting at the long table, with great dignity. The act was wasted because the prefect, busily making some notes, didn't so much as glance at them.

Jill went over to one of the windows, Nina following. They looked at each other inquiringly. "You," Nina whispered. "I've done my bit. I opened the box."

Jill tore open the envelope and removed the solitary sheet of paper. She'd been hoping the block letters were merely a coincidence, but she saw at once that this was an anonymous message similar to the others. But there was one great difference. This concerned herself. It said: THE CAPTAIN OF THE FOURTH HAS ENEMIES. THEY'LL WRECK HER PLANS FOR THE CONCERT.

In silence Jill passed the paper to Nina, who read it and scowled. "If I can only find out who sent this!" she hissed.

Jill said: "We'll talk about it later."

Jill found it hard to concentrate on the Elizabethan dramatists. She kept thinking of the message, wondering who sent it and whether there was any truth in it. The two earlier messages had been about Lindy, and they were true. So it suggested the mysterious writer was quite well-informed. But what was the purpose of the warning? To put her on her guard? Or to worry her? And Jill thought gloomily: It's certainly succeeding in that. It was so successful, in fact, that she fluffed her answer to a surprise question from Miss Latimer. There was a searching look from the mistress. She made no rebuke, but Jill was left feeling rather foolish.

When the lesson was over Jill breathed a sigh of relief. She turned to Nina, who occupied the next desk, and said: "I want fresh air."

They hurried down the broad steps of the main entrance and across to a vacant bench under one of the walnut trees. There was a brief silence, neither of them knowing quite what to say.

Eventually, Nina spoke. "It was intended for me. I mean, I'm the editor and everybody knows I have the key to the magazine box."

"But whoever sent it knows perfectly well that I help you with the mag and that, anyway, you'd tell me about a thing like this."

Nina nodded. "No secrets."

"No secrets," Jill confirmed.

"So the notes are addressed to me but intended for you."

"But why?"

Nina groaned. "Don't ask me—just don't ask me. The poor brain's going round in circles. Uselessly."

"The messages could be intended to help."

"And if you met a tiger in the woods it might be friendly." Nina shook her head. "Anyone who wanted to pass on a friendly warning would do it openly. This is secretive, anonymous, and nasty. My guess—it's a war of nerves."

"Why bring Lindy into the first two?"

"She's your worry, isn't she? I know you're not actually responsible for her; but form captains are encouraged to keep their own houses in order—if you see what I mean."

Jill nodded. Lindy, in her rebellious mood, was likely to be caught at any time and, while there would not be actual blame, there might be doubts of the form captain's suitability. It only needed one or two people to start saying that the Fourth seemed to be going to bits since Jill Rodgers became captain.

Jill said: "So somebody's trying to break my nerve."

"Seems that way to me," Nina said quietly. "If only I could think of a way of catching whoever's responsible! I'd commit assault and battery, so help me." She scowled ferociously. "But who?—who?—who? . . ."

Jill shook her head. "Let's forget it," she said wearily. "This way we're doing just what the unknown writer wants us to do—letting the thing get us down." She straightened up and looked around.

There were several girls in the large quadrangle, most of them near the school entrance. But Jill noticed that Judy Willets was hurrying in the direction of the school offices. She drew Nina's attention to this.

"You know we'll be getting a complaint, one of these days," Nina said. "Fourth form girls hovering around the bursar's office—etcetera! Judy's getting more and more pally with the new typist, Ann Page. Have you heard her showing off about it?"

"Can't say I have. What with the concert and everything else I've rather lost touch. What gives?"

Nina smiled. "Not much to tell. But can you see a
teenage girl in her first job really chumming up with
an empty-headed chatterbox like Judy? This Ann Page
must be a good-natured gal to take so much; but she'll
get fed up. Will she get fed up!"

"Have you suggested that to Judy?"

Nina laughed. "Not likely! It suits me. It's like
losing a sticking-plaster at long last."

Jill said: "The Bish is just coming out. Which reminds
me we're supposed to be writing a sketch for the concert.
We've no time for sitting here. Come on—get into the
act!"

Nina groaned. "Why did I ever tell you about my
cherished ambition to be a writer?"

"You've explained that," Jill said. "No secrets; just
as you said."

Beryl Bishop had come to the foot of the steps and was
glancing around. When she saw Jill and Nina she
strolled towards them. Wondering if this meant trouble,
they were a bit guarded; but the Bish was disarmingly
friendly.

"How's your stuff coming on for the concert?" she
asked.

"Stacks of suggestions," Jill said. "I think there are
four or five sketches being written. Out of those we'll
put forward the two best for the audition."

"Good work." There was a pause, then the Bish said:
"It's nice that something's going well!"

The fourth form girls looked at her inquiringly.

"I'm not giving away a secret, but all the same you'd
better keep this quiet until there's an official announcement. Long Field's definitely out."

"You mean the new owner's . . ." The exclamation came from Jill.

The Bish nodded. "Miss Garfield has been in touch with the Head. She wants the remains of the pavilion removed at once so that she can get work started on fencing off her property."

"Fencing it off!" Nina gasped.

"I'm afraid so. Men have already started to put up a high wire fence round the woods. So, any time at all, no end of our favourite walks and picnic places are going to be declared out of bounds."

"It's a miserable shame!" Jill said. "What damage have we ever done?"

The Bish sighed. "None, so far as I know. But that's it. Keep it to yourselves until it's made official."

"We will," Jill promised. "Thank you for telling us."

"I wish it could have been better news," the Bish said, and went on her way.

Jill and Nina walked a few steps in gloomy silence. Then Jill burst out with: "How can that Miss Garbage or whatever her name is be so unutterably mean?"

"What did Muriel call her? An ogre. Apart from having the gender wrong she was *so* right."

Jill asked: "Shall we put her in our sketch?"

"Muriel?"

"No, silly. Miss Gar—Garfield. Enter an ogress. How does that sound?"

"Too true to life," Nina answered grimly.

CHAPTER SIX

NINA TURNS PRIVATE EYE

IMMEDIATELY after prayers the next morning the Head made the announcement which Jill and Nina had hoped against hope would be averted by a last moment miracle. The news of Colonel Ashcroft's estate being under new ownership and now out of bounds, was received by the school in shocked silence. Afterwards, as a topic of conversation it thrust the concert far into the background.

Nina commented later in the day: "Miss Garfield's put herself right at the top of the unpopularity poll. I wonder what she's like?"

"As ugly as a rhino and about as pleasant," Muriel suggested. She'd spent her earliest years in Kenya and was the form's authority on wild life. Nobody disagreed with her comment, though Judy said as there was no accounting for tastes perhaps rhinos didn't see each other as ugly.

Muriel grinned and asked her what two rhinos had to do with Miss Garfield. It was a trap, of course, for Judy's explanations were always so painstakingly complicated that they could be relied on to provide a laugh. This time was no exception. She quickly reached the stage of absolute incoherence, led on by Muriel, with everyone around almost in hysterics.

"If you make fun of me how *can* I explain?" Judy demanded indignantly.

"Just what are you trying to explain anyway?" Muriel asked.

It suddenly dawned on Judy that she was being victim-ised. She grabbed the nearest cushion—they were in the common-room—and threw it at Muriel. She missed and hit Jill, who had just hurried in.

"I say, I'm frightfully sorry, Jill!" Judy began. "Do let me explain. . . ."

"Oh, no!" Nina gasped. "She's been doing that for the last five minutes, Jill. Please don't start her off again."

"Forget it, Judy," Jill said, smiling.

Judy looked relieved. Then she glared at the unre-pentant Muriel, said: "I'll go somewhere where the conversation's more intelligent," and swept out of the room.

Nina said quietly to Jill: "Bet she's gone to see Ann Page."

Jill sighed. "I wish Ann Page would send her packing. I suppose I ought to have a word with Judy; but it's tricky. I hate interfering, and I'm not a prefect."

"You wouldn't be interfering. You'd just be giving good advice."

"That's a wonderful way to win friends," Jill said. "Anyway, let's forget her for the time being. We've work ahead." She'd brought with her a foolscap folder which held the draft script of the sketch on which she was working with Nina. They took possession of a corner of the common-room and settled down to work. Gradually the room cleared and at last they were left alone.

"How long will this blessed state of peace endure?" Jill declaimed.

"A line for the sketch?" Nina asked.

"Nitwit! I'm talking of the quiet room."

"We can expect Vilma and Ruth. Not that they'll bother us; they'll be working on their effort. And I did hear they've asked Muriel to team up with them."

"Good idea. She'll be a help." Although Muriel was the form's pessimist, that was largely an act, and she could be very amusing.

Nina looked at her watch, jumped up and hurried out, leaving Jill staring after her in surprise. Nina was back within seconds.

"What was that in aid of?" Jill demanded.

Instead of replying immediately Nina sat down, took a diary from her cardigan pocket, and made a note in it.

"How many guesses do I get?" Jill asked.

"None." Nina was very serious. "I'm keeping an eye on the mag box."

Jill had noticed Nina going to the box several times during the day. She said: "I could still bear to be told." Nina leaned towards her, lowering her voice. "It's the beastly mystery notes. There'll be another, for sure. If I can possibly get an idea of *when* it's slipped into the box I can start checking where various people were at the time."

"Private eye stuff! But Nina, what an undertaking."

"How else are we to find who's responsible?"

"I don't know. But suppose we've been taking it all much too seriously? Perhaps it was a rather nasty joke and there'll be no more of it."

"You don't honestly believe that," Nina declared. She'd been doing a lot of careful thinking and now she explained her theories. They'd already considered the possibility that the messages might be a war of nerves, just to shake Jill's confidence. But there could be more to it. The messages about Lindy had been true. Perhaps they'd been sent simply for the purpose of making it seem the unknown sender was quite well informed.

Nina said: "So because the first two were true we tend to think the third must be. But it doesn't follow."

"You could be right," Jill agreed. "I've thought a bit on those lines myself. But you feel certain there'll be more of the horrid things and that they'll all be directed against me?"

"That's about it," Nina said. "A campaign to get you so badly rattled that you'll make mistakes. And we could be up against more than the anonymous messages."

"Meaning?"

"You get warnings, but nothing happens—so you finish up ignoring the messages. Sent by some crank. Get the idea? But if the writer means to be taken seriously, then things just have to go wrong."

"In what way?"

Nina sighed. "I wish I knew. I should think there'll be incidents that'll make for bad feeling—particularly between you and Vilma."

"I can't think Vilma would have anything to do with that sort of thing."

"Neither can I. But how about one of her close friends? Someone being over-partisan?"

"Like Ruth, for instance?" Jill shook her head. "I'd hate to think that Ruth . . ."

"The only way to put an end to perfectly horrid doubts is to find the culprit," Nina said firmly.

"Which is going to be tricky."

"There's always the chance of a stroke of luck." Nina didn't say any more, because the door opened and Vilma came into the common-room, followed by Ruth and Muriel.

The other two girls sat down, but Vilma came to the small table where Jill and Nina were working.

"We won't be disturbing you?"

"Of course not," Jill said. "Anyway, you've as much right to work in here as we have. It's the sketch, I suppose?"

Vilma nodded. "I've been wondering. We can put up two possibles to the selection committee. Who decides which two?"

Jill had already been thinking of this problem. The committee would decide on the final programme, but there had to be some preliminary weeding out. So far no arrangements had been made.

She said: "We could assemble the form, have each sketch read and then vote. Or we would pick an independent judge to read the scripts. Miss Stubbins, I suppose, as she's English mistress."

Nina groaned. "She's too square. I'll tell you one thing—our masterpiece is right out if she has any say."

"Top secret?" Vilma asked. "If you care to give, I will, too."

Nina glanced swiftly at Jill, who nodded, and then said: "We're not doing Shakespeare in modern dress, but Shakespeare in modern idiom. A scene from *As You Dig It*."

Vilma laughed. "Stubby's heart wouldn't stand it. Ours would be lethal, too. Spacemen land on Venus to find it really is Venus Land—but the goddess is ultra-modern, a bespectacled bio-chemist."

"Gorgeous!" Jill grinned. "I think with these we could take over the concert. But could the audience take it?"

"We could set aside a recovery room," Nina suggested.

Vilma said: "We're agreed? Not Miss Stubbins?" Hearing the door open she turned sharply. Seeing that it was only Judy Willets she looked at Jill again and said: "I wonder if we could go to Miss Latimer. After all, she's form mistress."

"Stubby might feel a bit slighted," Jill replied doubtfully.

"Don't forget she's suffering a bad cold," Nina suggested. "We wouldn't want to trouble her while she's under the weather."

"I say!" Judy had joined them.

Jill checked her. "Half a sec, Judy. Let me get this settled. Okay, Vilma. We'll ask Miss Latimer. She's taking prep to-night. Easy to speak to her afterwards. Will you join me?"

Vilma hesitated, shook her head. "I'm content to leave it to you," she said and started to move away; but Judy grabbed her arm.

Still holding Vilma, Judy exclaimed: "Listen! I want to tell you some news."

"Another rumour?" Vilma asked.

"It's not a rumour!" Judy was indignant. "I've just been told by Ann Page. The Head wrote to Miss Garfield, inviting her to tea and to look over the school, and would you believe it?"

"Believe what," Nina prompted.

"Miss Garfield refused. Ann says it was ever such a blunt letter—almost rude. Miss Garfield doesn't intend to have anything to do with the school. She's not able to accept any invitations."

"Coo-er!" Vilma gasped.

Jill frowned. "Judy," she said, knowing this was something she couldn't allow to slip by as harmless gossip, "I'm sure Ann Page shouldn't have told you that. It's the Head's business and shouldn't be repeated to anybody. Take my advice and forget it."

"But doesn't it just show what the old witch is like!"
Judy said excitedly.

"It does," Jill agreed. "But I still think . . ."

Vilma broke in. "Jill's right, Judy. Spread that story
and you'll find yourself trying to explain things to the
Head."

"Gosh!" Judy was really scared. "I'll keep quiet.
Honestly, I will."

Nina leaned back in her chair, looking thoughtfully
at Vilma. This wasn't the first time Vilma had openly
stood up for Jill. Was she being extremely sporting—or
was it calculated? Honest—or an act? Nina wished she
knew the answer.

CHAPTER SEVEN

AN ACCIDENT

WHEN the next half-day arrived, Jill went into town,
having insisted that Nina should accompany her. Nina
was reluctant because, in spite of the close attention she
was giving to the magazine box, she'd learned nothing.
"The instant my back's turned the creature's going to
push another nasty little message through that slot," she
declared.

"There hasn't been one so far. I really do begin to
think it was all a stupid joke that's worn itself out." Jill
wasn't quite so confident, though, as she made out.

Nina shook her head. "I've a thing about this. I know
I'm right, Jill. It isn't a joke."

"Suppose you *are* right and there's a note popped into
the box. You can still do a spot of teckery. It won't be

any of the girls on our bus or who are in town before we get there."

"Unless it's someone who sneaks back ahead of us." Nina wasn't to be comforted on this issue.

"I'm not going to have you camping in the corridor all afternoon," Jill insisted firmly. "You need a change." She laughed. "Besides, I claim a cream tea. In return for a sports article."

"Lucky for you I'm in funds," Nina said finally, surrendering. "A registered envelope this morning from Mother. Five lines of scribble to tell me she's had an oil painting hung in a local exhibition. It seems to have won some sort of prize. Anyway, she enclosed two pounds."

"How very nice!" Jill had the rather wistful thought that it must be exciting to receive unexpected gifts. Her father was a doctor and too immersed in his work to remember there were such things as presents. However, he gave her a reasonable allowance; but it was always sent to her by his secretary and that made it less personal and seemed to rob it of something.

Because of the time spent in persuading Nina to abandon her vigilance over the magazine box, they only just caught the bus. Jill leaned back to enjoy looking out of the window but Nina, still sleuthing, was busy making mental notes of which girls were on the bus.

They had a very busy half-hour in town doing oddments of shopping, including the purchase of more paper for their sketch. This was still in rough draft.

"Are you sure," Nina asked, as they sat at a window table in the café, "that what we've written can all be run through in twelve minutes?"

"I borrowed a stop-watch from Miss Frant, read at

a reasonable pace, and allowed for actions. Twelve minutes."

"And think how long it's taken to write! But the task's nearly over. We should complete the polishing up next session."

"There's still the typing."

"I can manage that." Nina was a fairly quick and accurate typist. Apart from having a small portable typewriter at home, she was always allowed to use a school machine for preparing the magazine stencil.

Remembering this, Jill said: "Do we stencil or just take carbon copies?"

"Carbons. We can manage with just a few—and we may not need those!"

"Nonsense! This is the winning effort," Jill declared. "After all, you're the literary genius of the Fourth. A first every term. How d'you achieve it? I don't. . . ." She broke off, staring down into the street. "Quick! Look across the road—the girl on the back of that scooter!"

The café being on the first floor, they had a good view of the street. Nina, leaning forward, was able to get a glimpse of the girl who'd attracted Jill's attention. But it was only a glimpse. A white crash helmet and a light coloured raincoat. That was all. She turned to look questioningly at Jill.

"Lindy," Jill said, her voice troubled.

"Lindy! Are you sure?"

Jill nodded. "I spotted her as she came out of that coffee bar opposite here. You know how you can tell people by their walk or something."

"Glory! If she's going careering round on the pillion of some boy's scooter she'll probably get herself expelled. How can she be so crazy?"

"It's not as risky as it seems, you know." Jill had been thinking hard. "Who'd recognise her? A skid-lid—goggles—white raincoat—all borrowed, of course. It was sheer chance that I spotted her. All the same, I agree it's crazy."

"Jill, you'll have to do something about her."

"Wish I knew what. Why can't she have some close friend in the form, someone who's got influence?"

"That was Pam Ralston," Nina said. "Lindy thought the world of her. Trotted round like a pet poodle, perfectly happy."

"I know," Jill said. "And I always felt that Pam just —you know—put up with her. No, a bit more than that. Pam was a generous, giving sort." She sighed. "But what to do! You keep saying I should do something. But I'm beaten. Lindy won't listen to me—not really listen."

"I bet this means she's going to be back late."

"Sure thing. I suppose we must try to get her into school without being seen by a prefect. Last time she was late the rain helped her."

" I wonder if there'll be anyone on gate duty. I don't know who decides. It just seems to happen." Nina's attention returned to the cream bun on her plate. "Well, we can only do our best. If Lindy's caught, she's caught. No one to blame but herself."

"How can you coax someone who simply couldn't care less?"

It was an unanswerable question. Nina shook her head.

The two friends returned to school earlier than they usually did on half-days, and Nina lost no time in opening the magazine box. It was empty. Jill, standing watching, said: "There—what does that prove?"

Nina shook her head. "Perhaps that Miss Poison Pen is among the persons who went to town. But it might simply mean that there isn't another message ready yet."

Jill grinned. "You know I'm grateful for what you're trying to do, pal; but it seems to me you're getting nowhere fast. Push it right out of your mind and let's finish the sketch. There's only a bit to do."

"Okay. But I'm not giving up," Nina said with determination.

There were only three girls in the common-room, each busily writing letters. One of them was Judy, who broke off and hurried to greet Jill and Nina.

"Don't let us disturb you," Jill said, trying to be tactful. "Go ahead and finish your letter."

Judy looked sadly at her fingers. "Why do I always get ink on myself? It's on the letter as well, worse luck. But Uncle Max won't mind—he's marvellous."

"You writing to remind him of your birthday?" Nina asked, a little shocked by the possibility.

"No, he's wizard! I had a letter by the afternoon post. I was too utterly broke to go into town, and I was *so* depressed. Then his letter arrived. He thought I'd like to buy something in time for my birthday. Three fifteen-bob postal orders and he suggested I shouldn't cash them all at once."

"Wise man!" Nina said.

"He's saved me from absolute ruination," Judy explained."

"Then you finish the letter to him," Jill said. "And make sure it isn't just Thank You spread over a couple of lines."

"Oh, it's a newsy letter," Judy protested.

"Knowing some of your newsy efforts it should really startle him," Nina said with a laugh.

"Don't be so beastly." Judy returned to her place at one of the tables.

Going across to the corner where they intended to work on the script for the sketch, Nina said quietly: "Judy I can definitely eliminate. She's too scatter-brained, and the anonymous notes are too neat and blot-free."

"Couldn't agree more," Jill said.

They settled down, hoping there'd be no interruptions from Judy, and in this they were lucky. As soon as Judy had finished her letter she went out. At last Nina leaned back with a sigh of relief.

"Curtain!"

"Am I glad it's done!" Jill exclaimed.

"Done! What a hope! We go through it. Correct. Improve. Cut out dull bits. Put in some brighter ones."

"Oh no!" Jill raised protesting hands.

"Absolutely necessary," Nina insisted.

"Talk me into it to-morrow. I couldn't do any more now."

They collected the sheets of paper and placed them in the folder. "Shove it in the corner of that cupboard for now," Jill said. "I'm tired of looking at it, and it'll be okay there."

Nina obeyed, saying with a chuckle. "Poor old Jill! You've stuck it well, though."

When Nina sat down again Jill looked at her searchingly. "You've gone all serious. What's up? Don't tell me you've had another bright idea. I just couldn't take it!"

Nina shook her head. "Thinking about Lindy."

"I'd forgotten her," Jill admitted. "Oh dear, always trouble."

Nina managed a very dignified expression. "Overcoming difficulties makes character."

"I seem to have heard that before. Of course! It's the Head's prize-giving speech. She always works that bit in. I suppose she's right, but at the moment *my* character prefers to avoid the difficulties."

"You're out of luck. Have you worked out a plan for Lindy?"

Jill shook her head. "Not knowing when the wretched girl will be back how can I make any sort of plan? You know, much as I want to help Lindy I'm *not* going to hang around near the gates for the best part of the evening."

"I don't somehow think she'll be very late this time. She had a scare the other evening, and on fine days like this it's much more risky. So many people may be around."

When the time came the gates were locked by one of the prefects. Jill and Nina watched from the cover of one of the thick bushes.

"It would be Hilda Wighton," Jill said gloomily. " You can bet she'll be on the prowl, all ready to take names."

"And make a fuss afterwards. Are you born bossy—or does it grow on you?"

"Quiet! She's coming this way."

The girls, stooping low, moved round the bush so as to keep it as a screen between themselves and the prefect. There was a bad moment when Jill, too close to the leaves, made them rustle. Hilda Wighton stopped and looked round. Jill and Nina dropped even lower and held their breath. After a few seconds the prefect appeared to be satisfied and moved on.

Jill put a hand to her heart. "Phew! That sent me all

fluttery. I know we're not doing any harm here—but it'd be difficult to explain why we're behind a bush near the gates."

"Especially to a suspicious mind," Nina endorsed. "What next?"

Jill had already worked this out. She led the way across to the thick hedge and fencing which formed the boundary. A little distance along was an old tree, its lower part easily climbable, and from here it was possible to get a good view along the road.

"You watch for Hilda Wighton," Jill said, as she accepted a hoist.

So Nina stayed below, looking vigilantly towards the school buildings. Jill, at about hedge-top level, was well hidden. After a while she called down: "Nobody in sight yet."

"You can't stay up there for ever," Nina said. "Come down and try again later."

"Shall I? I *am* getting a bit cramped and there's the stump of a broken branch digging into my back."

"Come on, Jill—hurry! I'm sure Hilda Wighton will be doing the rounds again any minute." Nina was growing anxious. It was all very well trying to help Lindy. But why risk serious trouble themselves for a girl who was inclined to resent help and certainly wouldn't take advice? On the whole, perhaps it was better to leave her to fend for herself.

"Coming." Then, after a slight pause, Jill added: "No! I'll hold on. I can see her. Gosh! There's something wrong. She's limping—and wobbling a bit." Jill's voice became urgent. "Nip along to the side gate, pal. Keep watch there."

Nina could hear the swish of branches and a thud. She knew Jill had crossed the hedge-top and the fence and dropped into the road. She turned and ran to the main gates, then beyond them to the small gate at the side. It was the gardener's responsibility to attend to the locking of this but he was usually rather late and it was popularly supposed that sometimes it slipped his memory altogether. Fortunately, this time was no exception, and Nina was able to open the gate and go out to the road. Jill and Lindy were approaching, Jill supporting Lindy. The girl looked distinctly the worse for wear. One side of her face was grimy and she was limping badly.

"Whatever's happened?" Nina gasped as they reached the gate.

"She came off that scooter," Jill said. "Is the coast clear?"

"Yes." Nina looked at Lindy critically. Her left stocking was torn and smeared with blood, her left wrist and hand grazed. The left side of her face was so dirty it was impossible to even guess what damage there was. "She should be taken straight to matron," Nina declared.

"No—please, no!" Lindy wailed. "If she sees me I'll have to tell what happened."

"That's for certain," Jill said, taking most of Lindy's weight as she helped her through the gate. " I don't think there's any serious damage. We can cope, once we get her up to the dorm."

"Hide! Quick!" Nina hissed. She hadn't relaxed her vigilance and was a couple of paces ahead. Hilda Wighton was coming towards the main gates, this time with another prefect. Nina waved frantically at Jill, who pulled Lindy behind the nearest bush. Within seconds Nina joined them.

"Is the game up?" Jill whispered.

"I think we've a chance. Two prefects this time and they're deep in conversation."

"A good chance," Jill murmured. Hilda Wighton on her own might hang around, and they couldn't move on towards the school buildings without being seen. Having a friend with her she'd not be so likely to linger. In fact, things worked out even better than Jill had hoped.

Nina, keeping a lookout, reported: "They're not coming as far as the gates. They're turning away and going towards Big Hall."

"I know what it is!" Jill exclaimed. "Setting out the chairs. They're doing a mock trial to-morrow. Civics. Fifth and Sixth combined."

"How d'you know that?" Nina demanded.

"On the notice board." Jill turned anxiously to Lindy. "Sorry if I was a bit rough when I dragged you into hiding. You still okay?"

"A bit trembly. I've walked a long way. You see, the scooter packed up when we came to grief, and Tim couldn't just leave it there. I knew the time was getting on and I was scared of staying out any longer. Tim tried to thumb me a lift but the cars swept by."

"Just as well for you, as it happens," Jill said. "Don't worry. We'll soon have you more presentable. Coast clear yet, Nina?"

"Yes. Keep behind me."

Nina walked a few yards ahead, careful to take full advantage of the cover of the bushes. Just as Lindy had done on a previous occasion, they made use of the back stairs. It took them some time, because Lindy's injured leg was stiff and painful. However, luck was with them and they passed matron's quarters undetected. They were equally lucky when they came to the stairs leading up to the dormitory, for the door of the common-room was closed and the corridor deserted.

"Am I thankful that's over!" Nina exclaimed, as they reached the comparative safety of the dormitory. They got Lindy to her bed, then Nina collected sponge and towel while Jill inspected the damage.

"You were lucky," Jill declared. "Nothing worse than a few scratches."

"Even my leg?" Lindy sounded doubtful.

"It's not a deep cut," Jill assured her. She proceeded efficiently with cleaning away the dirt. Nina, meanwhile, had raided the nearest first-aid box.

When Jill had finished, Lindy said: "You're awfully good at this sort of thing, aren't you?"

"That's having a doctor for a father," Jill said. "I've often helped him with little things like this. Actually, too, there've been two occasions when we were out on pleasure and came on the scene of nasty road accidents—much worse than falling off a scooter—and I helped with the injured."

"Goodness! You've learned so much—and yet you want to waste it all by being a vet," Lindy said, puzzled.

"*You're* a fine one to talk about not using talents the right way," Nina said indignantly.

For once, Lindy seemed a little shame-faced. "Sorry—I—I didn't mean . . ."

"Okay. Skip it, for the moment." Jill was busily dabbing a special soothing lotion of her own on to tender parts of Lindy's skin that were still exposed. "A lot of what I've learnt will come in useful, Lindy, and it's a good thing for everyone to know a bit of first-aid. That feel better?"

"Much, thanks, Jill. Only a bit shaky.

"Cocoa time, now. Hot drink and plenty of sugar—

and you'll feel fine. Think you can make it down to the common room?"

Lindy nodded. "I think so. I was more scared than really hurt, I think. I got in a panic and I was bleeding. . . ."

"You'll probably have to own up to having a fall, to account for the plaster and the scratches."

"I'll do that. You've been jolly decent, Jill. And Nina, too. Thanks."

"Perhaps you can show a bit of practical gratitude," Nina suggested. "Stop playing up. You'll make life easier for yourself—and for a few others."

"It's easy for you to talk. You're—well, you're still content with school and kid-stuff. It's so—so—futile and I'm in a hurry to start doing all the things you can do when you leave school. And . . ."

"In so much of a hurry you don't mind getting expelled?" Jill asked quietly.

Lindy stared at her. "No—not really. When I think that may happen I get afraid." She pushed her hands through her hair. "I suppose I'm all mixed up."

"You can say that again," Nina murmured.

CHAPTER EIGHT

STRANGE BEHAVIOUR

AFTER HER misadventure Lindy was rather subdued; but there was nothing to suggest that she intended to change her ways. Nina said wearily: "Only a matter of time before we get ourselves involved in another rescue operation. You know, the silly bighead's lucky that you're captain. Vilma would never have the patience."

"Mine's wearing thin," Jill confessed.

They'd had permission to type out their sketch. There was a room used for secretarial training and it was part of the office block. Miss Latimer had told them to ask the bursar for the key. However, it was Ann Page who unlocked the door for them.

"You're to use that typewriter," she said, pointing to one of the machines. She was distinctly curt in manner.

"Thank you." Jill would have said more, but Ann Page swung round and hurried out, saying over her shoulder: "When you're through, lock the door and drop the key into my office."

As soon as they were alone Nina grimaced. "You get the message the way I did—that she's not friendly?"

Jill nodded. "Can't think why." She'd seen the bursar's typist in the distance but this had been her first encounter with the girl, who was quite an attractive blonde though her appearance was marred by a tight-lipped expression.

"I'd have thought she was putting on airs for the benefit of mere schoolgirls," Nina said. "But how do you explain Judy?"

"I don't." Jill shrugged her shoulders. "I don't care much, either. If she wants to be upstage, let her. We've a job to do, remember?"

Nina removed the cover from a typewriter. "Four copies, I think. There's a song—that can be typed separately."

"I'll do it on another machine," Jill offered. "It'll be okay. That girl was only showing off when she issued orders. My one-finger speed'll just about get the song done for when you've finished the play."

"About time you learned to type properly," Nina said.

"Anyhow, get cracking." She handed over the draft of the song.

Jill's typing wasn't nearly so elementary as she made out and she was able to lend a hand with the bigger task. When all was done, they put the typed copies in the folder with the original draft, tidied up, and left. Jill locked the door and they crossed to Ann Page's office to return the key. They paused outside, hearing laughter.

"That's Judy," said Nina.

She was right. Evidently the bursar was out. Ann Page was sitting sideways at her desk, applying nail enamel. Judy sat on a table, swinging her legs.

Ann Page looked up as they entered.

"We're through, thanks," Jill said, determined to be as pleasant as possible. "We've left it all quite tidy."

"Just drop the key." Ann Page spoke as curtly as before.

"You giving tennis a miss, Judy?" Nina asked.

"It's cancelled. Didn't you know?"

"We certainly didn't," Jill said. "When was this?"

"Nearly an hour ago—perhaps not quite so long—due to old Mangold-wurzel. He got the days and the times mixed up and gave the courts a thorough watering."

"Brilliant!" This was a disappointment to Jill. She'd been looking forward to a practice game with Nina after the typing task was over.

Nina was equally disappointed. As they left the offices she said: "This term, things always seem to be going wrong! Muriel says a steady disintegration has set in. She's taken the age of the school and the month when it was opened and got hold of some what-the-stars-foretell gen. It's real Cassandra stuff."

"Cassandra?"

"You know! She foretold the doom of Troy, but

nobody would believe her. In the end Agamemnon's wife killed her. Greek mythology. Sordid passage."

Jill laughed. "Aren't they all? Yes, I remember now. Don't know that I feel sorry for her; people who spread gloom are awfully trying."

"Tell that to Muriel!"

They went up to the common-room. Vilma Blake was there, writing a letter. "You've heard about the tennis?" she asked.

"Just," Jill told her. "We got it from Judy, so I won't answer for its being accurate."

From what Vilma said it seemed Judy's version was more or less correct. She finished by saying: "Miss Frant's pretty mad about it. I heard her mutter: ' That stupid old man never listens to anything! '"

"Has something been organised instead of tennis?" Nina asked.

Vilma spread out her hands. "I think Miss Frant was too put out to give it a thought. Too late to do anything now and the girls have scattered, so it becomes an extra half-day, doesn't it? Matter of fact, it's just a nuisance to me as it happens. I wanted to get in some hard practice. That St. Hilda's match is coming nearer and nearer."

"We'll pull it off," said Jill encouragingly. She turned to Nina. "Well—what do we do?"

Ruth and Denise came into the common room. They went straight to Vilma. "Haven't you finished that silly old letter yet?" Ruth demanded.

Nina said to Jill: "Let's go for a walk—away from it all." She was carrying the folder. "Shall I take this up to my locker in the dorm?"

"Leave it," Jill suggested. "We've put it in the cupboard often enough."

Nina put it away and they went out, leaving a protesting Vilma trying to convince Ruth and Denise that her letter really was important and must be finished before she did anything else.

The two friends were soon going through the gates and along the road to a stile which was the start of a route across some fields.

"I suppose this is okay," Nina said. "Officially, it's a sports afternoon, but . . ."

"We're taking exercise," Jill said. "Better than hanging around in school doing nothing." She looked wistfully towards the inviting mass of the woods. "If only . . . Oh, what's the use!"

"Why did the wretched woman have to move in so quickly? It was almost like turning the poor old colonel out."

"I should think the deal must have been coming off for quite some time," Jill replied. "Only the colonel didn't say anything until the last minute. Maybe he still hoped there was a chance of saving the place. I'm sure he loved it."

"It must've been a frightful blow. Look how he reacted to that suggestion of a farewell party for him —just to thank him for all he'd done for Hazelmere in the past."

Jill nodded. Nobody was quite sure what the colonel had written to the Head when he'd expressed regret at not being able to accept the invitation; but the opinion was that he'd felt it would be too misery-making for him.

Instead of taking a path leading towards the woods, the girls went straight on. The trimness of the cultivated fields gave way to gorse-bush untidiness of a broad stretch of common. It was pleasant enough, but not comparable with the land belonging to the adjoining estate which the colonel had owned.

"We'll have to make the best of this in future," Jill said. "I wish it wasn't right up against the smaller of the woods," Nina commented. "It's a constant reminder of what we've lost. A bit tempting, too."

"Yes. I'm so sore about it all that I'd take a delight in trespassing. It wouldn't do, though. I bet if Miss Garbagey Garfield found anything like that was happening she'd make all the trouble she could."

"Probably want the offenders put into the stocks—loaned from the town museum for the occasion."

"Let's talk about something more pleasant," Nina said.

"Like the way Ann Page behaved, for example. She couldn't have been more frigid to us—yet she was chattering amiably to Judy. I don't get it."

"I almost have the impression that Judy's been stuffing her up with stories about us. You know—putting her against us. Only I can't quite believe that. Anyway, we've never harmed Judy, so why should she? And she's not the sort to make mischief—not deliberately."

"Perhaps Ann Page improves as you get to know her better," Jill suggested. She stopped and listened. "I can hear some dogs somewhere. Joyously excited."

"Remember the colonel's gorgeous red setter? Hope he's still able to live in the country."

"Not the dog for a town flat," Jill agreed. "Remember that sports day when he managed to slip away from the colonel and got into the refreshment tent? Stood near a low trestle table, wagged his tail, and whoosh! About three dozen cups and saucers went flying!"

Nina laughed. "I'll never forget it. He was sure he'd been clever, too."

"And the colonel was so nice about it. Insisted on paying for the damage and said: ' Wish old Rufus would do that to me sister's tea-service. I loathe it—cups have such darn stupid little handles.' It was a scream!"

Most of the trees on this stretch of common had been felled and there were still a few gnarled trunks left lying. Jill and Nina perched on one which was just the right height for a seat.

Jill said: "We've got to persuade ourselves this is a very good spot. Which, actually, it is; only I'm afraid no amount of pretending will make it seem as good as any of the places we've lost."

"Too true," Nina agreed. A rustling attracted her attention and she turned her head sharply. "Oh, look! One of the dogs we heard, I suppose."

"A sealyham," Jill said. "Hallo!" She slipped from the log and went towards the dog, moving steadily and talking to him quietly. She interjected an instruction to Nina that she was to stay absolutely still.

For a moment the dog growled and it seemed he would back away. Then he seemed to understand that Jill was friendly and waited. She'd seen at once that he was holding up a paw as if it pained him.

"Let me see, boy," she said, as she came very near.

The dog stiffened. Jill fearlessly kept her hand extended and steady. She went on talking, encouragingly. At last the dog made up his mind. He came forward awkwardly and licked her fingertips. A few minutes later he was content to let her kneel and pet him.

"Anything I can do to help?" Nina asked, approaching the dog and Jill very slowly, so as not to make the sealyham suspicious.

"Tell you in a minute," Jill said. She went on talking to the dog. "Now let's look at this foot of yours. What have you done to it?" Already she was feeling the bones, exploring with fingers that were not inexperienced.

"Nothing wrong. But I bet I know what. Steady now . . ." She moved the dog over slightly and gave an exclamation of satisfaction. "Yes! What I thought! Here's the trouble." She glanced at Nina. "A thorn— quite a nasty one and in rather deep."

"Can you cope?"

"Sure. I'd like a dab of antiseptic, but we'll have to do without. The secret is to be very steady and quick. There! That's done."

The dog wriggled his body gratefully and licked Jill's hand.

"And very neat, too!"

It was a strange voice. The girls turned quickly and saw that a woman was watching them. They hadn't heard her approach, which was surprising in view of her sturdiness. But if she could walk softly, there was nothing subdued about her voice.

"Hang on to his collar or he'll be off chasing imaginary rabbits again. You'll have to carry him. Well, don't squat there gawping at me, girl. Pick him up. Follow me." She moved towards a thick patch of bushes, calling loudly, evidently to the other dogs.

Jill and Nina exchanged glances of bewilderment. Then Jill said: "I suppose we do."

The dog snatched a lick at her face and at the same time the woman glanced back and called: "Hurry yourselves—or we'll lose all the others!"

"Nuts, of course," Nina murmured. "All right to carry the dog for her, I suppose, though."

CHAPTER NINE

IN THE ENEMY'S CAMP

NINA said, in a small, troubled voice: "I'm beginning to get a horrible suspicion."

They were still following the woman and were now nearing a gateway in the fence which ran along the edge of the wood. She was about twenty yards ahead of them and she'd succeeded in calling up the dogs. There were four of them. The largest, an airedale, was apparently called Gulliver. There was a black spaniel who'd reluctantly answered to the name of Hector, a smooth dachshund and a peke.

Jill, still carrying the sealyham who seemed perfectly content with this arrangement, sighed and said: "So you think so, too."

"Who else could she be? She's a stranger—we've never seen her before. She's got a bullying way that just ties up with taking our sports field and closing the woods against us."

"On top of which we're going towards a path that leads pretty straight through the wood to the house."

Nina said: "We'll soon know for certain. She's just coming to the gate. This is where she takes the dog from you and tells us to be good little girls and get back to school."

Jill gave her celebrated imitation of a growl. "Wouldn't I love to tell her just what the school thinks of her! Not that it'd do any good."

"Probably please her. I bet she gets a kick out of being disliked."

Jill's sense of fairness asserted itself. "All the same, she does seem to be fond of dogs. That must be a point in her favour."

Nina was not so sure. "Perhaps because they can't answer back," she said.

"Hurry up!" the woman called. "Through this gate!" She went through herself, just managing to grab Hector who'd had a sudden impulse to set off in a different direction.

"Not waiting for us!" Jill exclaimed. "Have we to go fagging all the way to the house. . . ."

"We get another look at our favourite wood," Nina said. "Though that may not be a good thing. Seeing what you've lost doesn't usually cheer you up, does it?"

"I think she's got a nerve!" Jill declared. "If I wasn't carrying the dog, I'd soon make myself scarce." Suddenly she laughed. "Still, we're going to have a fine tale to tell when we get back. Judy'll turn positively green. You know how she likes to be first with any news."

"With the wild rumour before the news," Nina corrected.

They came to the gate and passed through it. Miss Garfield—they were now certain they'd identified her correctly—was so far ahead that she was out of sight, but they could hear her calling to the dogs. Simon seemed to be giving her trouble. They weren't sure whether Simon was the dachs or the peke.

They finally overtook the dogs and their owner where the trees ended and there were ornamental bushes surrounded by closely clipped grass. Beyond was the house, not so large as the extensive estate suggested. Jill and Nina, like many girls from Hazelmere, had been inside. It had been the colonel's custom to give a party, as near to Christmas as the term ending permitted.

"Not too tired of carrying Barney? Not that he deserves such pampering. He's more trouble than all the others put together, which is saying a lot. Well, don't stand there. Come inside and we'll have some tea—that is, if I can persuade my simpleton of a Gertrude to make some." And well before she was at the porch she was calling to the luckless Gertrude.

Jill and Nina exchanged worried glances. "What do we do?" Nina whispered quickly.

"Wish I knew. I'd like to clear off; but it'd seem rude."

Nina nodded. "Bad policy. I suppose there's just a chance she might think again about the playing field. If so it'd be silly to offend her."

"Mmm. Tea with the enemy, though. It makes me feel a wee bit scared."

"Don't let her see that. It's maybe what she enjoys—scaring people. . . . Could be that her bark's worse than her bite, though. She yells at the dogs but it doesn't seem to worry them a scrap."

As if to encourage Jill, Barney contrived to give her another lick.

"Come along, girls. I'm not going to eat you!"

Jill and Nina looked at each other again, shook their heads rather despairingly, and made their way up the steps and into the house. There was a large, square hall, but they were called into the lounge. The room was very different from their last memory of it. Colonel Ashcroft had been neat and methodical and his rooms, even when specially arranged for a party, had looked tidy and orderly. Miss Garfield hadn't been in the place long but there was already absolute confusion.

"Dump your things anywhere," she said. She was already removing a shapeless hat which she threw on to a settee. She was wearing a tweed suit, the jacket of which she took off and flung near the hat. "I'm Miss Garfield," she announced, confirming their deduction. "Over there is Theodora."

Theodora was a sleek cat, sitting comfortably in a big arm-chair and regarding proceedings without any indication of interest.

Miss Garfield went to a large cage in which there was a grey parrot. "And this is Diogenes." She turned round quickly. "Know who Diogenes was?"

After only a moment's thought Nina said: "A Greek philosopher. He lived in Athens—in a tub."

"Good!" Miss Garfield exclaimed. "It's said he was rude to everybody." She shook a finger at the parrot. "That fits, you old scoundrel!"

The parrot leaned his head forward. "Yak—yak—yak! Old Ma Gee talks too much!"

Miss Garfield cackled with laughter. "What did I tell you?"

"Belt up!" the parrot yelled. There seemed to be wicked amusement in his small, shiny eyes.

The girls were having difficulty in preventing their polite smiles from becoming hearty laughter. Miss Garfield looked hard at them and then grinned warmly. "Oh, don't mind me." She swept some papers and magazines from a small table and suddenly yelled: "Gertrude! Are you doing anything about that tea?"

There was no reply.

"Sulking, I expect," Miss Garfield said. "She does, when I shout at her. But she *sniffs* at me—that's worse. What are your names?"

The girls introduced themselves. Miss Garfield nodded. "And you're from Hazelmere?" When the girls told her this was so, she said: "I was invited to something or other. Can't remember what. But I refused. I always do. I'm no good at parties."

"Ma Gee!" the parrot shouted. "Yak-yak-yak." He cocked his head to one side and appeared to be studying Miss Garfield thoughtfully. Finally, in a lower tone, he said: "Get lost!"

Miss Garfield glared at him. "They say parrots just repeat what they've picked up, without knowing the meaning. Stuff! This wicked old sinner knows exactly what he's saying."

Diogenes ignored her. He was busy scratching his head. A middle-aged woman, tall and thin with a lean face, came into the room carrying a tea-tray. She placed it on the table.

"I'll bring the tea as soon as the kettle's boiled," she said.

Jill and Nina had been feeling rather sorry for Gertrude; but assuming this was she, they realised their sympathy was wasted. Gertrude could look after herself.

"No *cherry* cake?" Miss Garfield demanded after inspecting the load on the tray.

"You finished that yesterday. Three slices."

"I expect I was hungry," Miss Garfield said.

Gertrude sniffed loudly and went out.

"You've had it!" Diogenes announced.

Miss Garfield shook a fist at him. Then she said: "Sit down, girls. Bring up chairs. If there's anything on them, tip it off. But don't disturb Theodora. She'll sulk. Kept it up for a week once—just looked straight through me every time. Do you know, I had to apologise in the end? Yes—apologise!" She looked critically at Jill. "You pulled that thorn out of Barney's foot very expertly."

"I want to be a vet," Jill explained. "And during the

hols I always manage to put in quite a lot of time helping Captain Barry. He's a vet who lives near to us."

"I see." Miss Garfield appeared interested. So interested that she had no complaints when Gertrude brought in the tea. Indeed, she didn't speak again until she'd passed them their cups. Then she fired a question. "Suppose you had to give some medicine to a dog and it was a medicine you also give to humans. You know the adult dose but you've not been told what to give to a dog. How much would you give?"

"For an average-sized dog about the same," Jill said.

"Suppose you had to treat a cat?"

"Roughly half what I'd give a dog."

Miss Garfield nodded. "Excellent. Help yourself to eats. I don't know what's in the sandwiches. It might be salmon. Try one and tell me."

Nina shook her head. "This is sardine and cucumber. And it's delicious."

"That woman will not give me salmon sandwiches," Miss Garfield complained. She leaned forward. "Know why?"

Nina shook her head.

"Secretly she absolutely adores Theodora. And Theodora adores salmon. So *I* get sardine sandwiches." Miss Garfield turned to Jill. "How many teeth does a cat have?"

"Thirty," Jill said.

"Quite right. Have another sandwich."

"I've not finished this one yet, thank you."

"Have another one when you have." Miss Garfield looked at Nina. "And what are you going to do when you leave school?"

"I'd like to work on a magazine—or for a publisher."

"Nina edits our magazine," Jill said. "A special one just for the fourth form. Two issues a term."

"Send me a copy," Miss Garfield instructed. "Another sandwich, Nina?"

"No, thank you."

"Then try the cake. Tell me if there's peel in it. I can't bear candied peel and she puts it in just to spite me."

"Ma Gee—get lost!" Diogenes shrieked.

"I'll turn you loose in the bird sanctuary. The others'll mob you and then *you'll* be lost," Miss Garfield retorted.

"Bird sanctuary?" Jill repeated.

"Yes. Can you think of anything better to do with a couple of woods? They're ideal." Suddenly Miss Garfield became very serious as she told them she had a great friend who was expert at filming wild life. Once the two sanctuaries were established this friend would be coming down to do some filming.

"So that's why you're putting up high wire fencing," Jill said thoughtfully.

"Of course. And it's proving mighty expensive. There are some fields to fence, too—for the horses."

"Horses, Miss Garfield?" Nina asked.

"Old horses. Those whose working days are over and who'd be put to sleep. Some friends help me out—we buy them and give them a quiet retirement." She laughed. "They thrive on it, too. One's been with me for seven years and he's still going strong. You'll see him. I'm having them all brought here. At the moment they're scattered. We've three fields, all quite a distance apart."

"It'll be much more convenient," Jill agreed.

"Hurry up and get started as a vet. You'll be useful." When, at last, the strange tea-party was over, Jill and

Nina went back through the woods in thoughtful silence. At last Nina said: "She's not nearly so awful as I thought at first. In fact she's rather—well, she's not a bad sort."

"Mmm," said Jill slowly. Was she, she wondered, being disloyal to the school in having taken a liking to the odd Miss Garfield?

There was silence for a few minutes. Then Nina said: "Of course, you made a good impression—pulling out that thorn—then when she pelted you with questions and you gave the right answers. I wonder . . ."

Jill nodded. "I know what you're thinking. Ought I to have appealed to her about the sports field? I did wonder, pal. And I just couldn't make up my mind."

"She's not like most people. No knowing how she'd take it. Perhaps you did the right thing in keeping quiet. To have started asking favours within half an hour of meeting her—yes, it could have seemed a bit much."

"Perhaps there'll be a better chance," Jill said, without any real hope.

"Meanwhile," Nina said, "I suggest we keep absolutely quiet about all this. The others wouldn't understand. They'd blame us for not taking a chance."

"I get the message," Jill said, and she didn't admit even to Nina that she felt this had been perhaps her biggest failure as captain of the Fourth.

CHAPTER TEN

A SHOCK

NINA looked up, bewildered. She was stooping at the cupboard in the common-room.

"Jill! It isn't here!" she exclaimed.

It was the day following their meeting with Miss Garfield. They'd returned to school with so much on their minds that they'd forgotten all about the folder containing the sketch for the concert. And now that they had remembered, it wasn't there.

"It must be," Jill said. "You put it in there just before we went out yesterday. I think I suggested you should, because—well, we'd done that often enough while we were writing it, anyway."

Nina straightened up. "It's not here now. Jill, this is dreadful! Do you realise that there were the typed copies and the original draft *and* all our notes in the folder? If it doesn't turn up we can't . . . we just can't possibly start again from scratch!"

"Easy, pal. Of course it'll turn up. No point in getting rattled." Jill wasn't feeling any too calm herself, but she made a great effort to hide this. "First of all, let's make absolutely sure, shall we? You've looked—now I'll look."

"It's all yours," Nina said, standing aside.

She watched as Jill looked through the stacks of magazines and odd papers which were kept on the lowest shelf of the cupboard. Jill did the job thoroughly, making sure nothing had fallen down at the back. This done she stood up. "We put it there—it's not there now," she said slowly. "So somebody's taken it. Who? Why?"

"I wish you'd answer questions instead of asking so many," Nina commented. She thought for a moment. "A joke?"

"Not a very intelligent one."

"I can name a few girls in the Fourth who aren't very intelligent," Nina murmured.

"Never mind that," Jill said quickly. "Let's assume it's a joke." Inwardly she wasn't so sure. A joke was done for fun, even if the fun was a bit corny. But what if malice entered into it? Then it wasn't a joke any longer. Not at all funny. Somebody trying to make her look foolish? Part of a sly campaign to get someone else elected as form captain?

"Let's try to reason it," Nina said. "Did anyone know that we put the folder here?" She nodded. "Sure. Vilma was around—and Ruth—and Denise." She considered this and shook her head. "I don't think practical jokes, especially feeble practical jokes, are in their line." She shook her head again. "No, I'd put them in the clear."

Jill reminded her that no one else had been in the room at the time. "Not," she said, "that that proves anything. After all, someone going to the cupboard might have found the folder."

"I was getting around to that myself," Nina said. "Three people could actually have seen me put it away—the rest could have happened on it by chance." She grimaced. "Helpful, isn't it?"

"Much more helpful if we'd remembered the sketch when we came in yesterday—instead of thinking about Miss Garfield and whether we should've asked her about the sports field."

"There was prep, too," Nina pointed out. "That pulled our thoughts in another direction."

"Don't remind me! If there's one thing that puts me off it's being glared at."

"That's the odd thing about Miss Pringel. I bet you could ask all round the form and every girl would swear Miss Pringel was glaring at her all the time. And she only gives that impression—I'm sure she doesn't mean it. It comes from dealing with the tiresome brats in the second form." Miss Pringel was form mistress of the Second.

Jill said slowly: "It could be important that Miss Pringel took prep."

Nina looked puzzled. "Doesn't make sense to me."

"It narrows down the time. Nobody ever tries to go out during prep or to finish up earlier when Miss P. takes it."

Nina frowned, concentrating. "There were no absences at supper, and I don't think anybody was late going to bed." She brightened up. "Jill—something for certain—the whole form wouldn't be in on this."

"So?"

"Somebody may have noticed something; vaguely, I mean. I'd say some discreet questioning's indicated." Nina looked hard at Jill. "You're awfully solemn; and I mean awfully."

"You can say that again." Jill hesitated, then plunged. "It could be very much not a joke, Nina."

"You mean somebody would be mean enough to deliberately . . ." Nina began, with instinctive disbelief. Then she stopped, scowled and said: "Yes, they might be at that."

Jill said: "I think we're in an awkward position, pal." To take any official action, such as reporting the loss to

Miss Latimer, would be too much like tale-bearing. Yet to call a form meeting and challenge the culprit to come out into the open, might look like a sort of declaration of war on Vilma Blake, and this was the very thing Jill was most anxious to avoid.

She explained her views to Nina, who agreed completely, saying: "I think we carry on with my idea of discreet inquiries and see what we can unearth. Right?" And Jill nodded.

This took place at the mid-morning period between lessons and they'd become so preoccupied that they were only just able to reach the science lab in time for the next lesson.

Jill wasn't able to dismiss the problem from her mind. She found herself looking at various girls suspiciously. It was an uncomfortable experience and she was very relieved when the bell rang.

As they returned to their form room Nina whispered: "Only geography to go, then we can start asking some questions."

Jill was normally good at geography but this time was the exception and towards the end she had merely the vaguest idea of the mountain system of North Africa. She barely scraped through when Miss Latimer asked her on which side of the Tell Atlas were there fertile terraces.

"Phew! I'm glad that's over," she confided to Nina. "If you hadn't done that swimming mime I'd never have answered the last question. My head just wasn't clear enough to realise all the fertile land's on the seaward side. I was still tangled up in wondering who's taken our folder."

"I wasn't much better myself," Nina confessed. Abandoning the idea that the sketch had been taken for a joke, she'd been trying to work out who might have done it with the deliberate intention of creating difficulties for Jill. Rather reluctantly she'd decided Ruth Tranter was the top suspect. Ruth was so fanatically pro-Vilma. If this was right, would Ruth confide in Vilma? Watching them both, Nina had become convinced that something was wrong. Ruth was looking quite downcast and Vilma looked stormy.

What had happened?

Nina wasn't left wondering for long, because just outside the common room Jill caught Judy's arm.

"I want to talk to you, Judy."

Judy Willets was instantly alarmed. "It isn't . . . I haven't done anything wrong, have I, Jill?"

Jill grinned. "I wouldn't know."

"I always intend to do the right thing. You know— for the best," Judy said earnestly.

"I'm sure," Nina said dryly.

All the other girls had disappeared by now, so the three were alone. Judy turned to Nina and complained: "I don't like the way you said that, Nina. Have you still got it in for me over that little mistake in my gossip stuff for the mag?"

"That's forgotten," Nina assured her.

Jill said: "Judy. If I tell you something, can you manage to keep quiet about it? *Really* quiet, I mean?"

Judy was obviously most intrigued. "Oh, I say! Is it a secret? You can trust me—honestly you can, Jill. I won't breathe a word."

"Good," Jill said briskly. She told Judy about the missing folder.

"Gosh!" Judy was genuinely astonished. "All that work you did—all the typing? Oh, no!"

"I'm afraid it's ' Oh, yes,'" Jill said.

"But who'd pinch it?" Judy demanded.

"We wondered if you'd heard anything," Jill replied.

"You're so often first with the news," Nina remarked.

Judy shook her head. "Of course, if anyone *did* pinch it they'd be dead silent, wouldn't they?"

"Might not," said Nina. "Suppose it was done for a joke. A joke rather does have to be shared, doesn't it?"

"I haven't heard the tiniest rumour," Judy said. Then her eyes widened. "There *was* a dreadful row about it."

"A row?" Jill asked sharply.

Nina moved closer. "Tell, Judy," she said.

"I was only in on it by chance," Judy responded, lowering her voice and clearly preparing to enjoy herself. "I came up to the common-room and there were only three people in there. Vilma, Denise, and Ruth. Vilma was finishing a letter."

Jill and Nina exchanged glances. This must have been shortly after they'd left the common-room and set out on their walk.

Judy continued: "Denise was looking at a record catalogue . . ." And Ruth, according to her story, was by the cupboard. Vilma finished her letter and then asked Ruth what she was reading. Ruth showed the folder and said she was taking a peep at the sketch most likely to compete with their own.

"Do you know," Judy said, "Vilma blew her top! Phew! She went up like a space rocket. Told Ruth off for snooping and made her put the folder back. Ruth was too surprised to do more than stammer and stutter. Denise tried to make peace by saying no harm was done, and was told to keep out of it. Ruth went as red as fire and said she was sorry. She put the folder back and then marched out. I don't know whether they made it up later. I was—well, I was busy."

Nina said: "You're sure Ruth *did* put the folder back?"

"Absolutely certain. And Vilma stood over her, making sure she did it."

"Thanks for the information, Judy," Jill said. "Mind you keep the loss of the folder to yourself. Remember your promise."

"Cross my heart. *And* I'll keep eyes and ears open. If I learn anything I'll let you know at once."

"Don't go all mysterious over questioning people, will you?" Nina warned.

Judy looked offended. "I know how to keep a still tongue in my head. I'll show you, Miss Cassel."

"Delighted to be shown," Nina retorted.

When Judy had bustled into the common-room, the two friends went along to the library. Fortunately, it was deserted. They sat near one of the windows and talked quietly. Judy's story was very interesting but they realised they must accept it with caution. It was almost certain to be exaggerated.

"But Ruth does look miserable and Vilma's got that on-the-warpath appearance," Nina said.

Jill thought they could take for granted that Ruth had peeped at their sketch and Vilma had stoppped her. "I'm not so sure there was anything of a scene," she said. "Maybe. Maybe not. The question is, did Ruth make up her mind to have another look—a really good look— at our effort? Did she borrow it and then for some reason fail to put it back?"

Nina considered the possibility. "I can't see Ruth hanging on to it, either for a joke or for a nastier reason. But it could be she was tempted to get a preview of the opposition. After all, she's helping Vilma and they're quite likely to produce something as good as our master-piece." She smiled. "I could bear to see how *theirs* is going. Well—Ruth has borrowed it and hasn't had a chance of putting it back. That might be why she's looking unhappy. And she can't ask Vilma for help, because she's already been in disgrace for snooping."

Jill nodded. "It's possible. Now if the theory's right, we have to make it easy for Ruth. But how?"

"That question's twisting my brain into knots," Nina admitted. "We can hardly put a notice on the board, offering to help anyone who wishes to return our sketch to the common-room. . . ."

"Talking of the common-room, let's go there right now," Jill said. "Just as well not to look as though we're hatching a plot—as it could if someone came in here."

As they went along the corridor Nina stopped by the magazine box. She fumbled for the key. "I've been slipping, Jill. So much else has happened that the watch system's broken down. This'll be the first inspection to-day." She had the box open and her face became serious as she took out an envelope. She tore it open and then, without a word, passed it to Jill. It was in the familiar block letters and read: HAVE JILL AND NINA LOST THE SKETCH THEY'D WRITTEN FOR THE CONCERT— OR IS THE TRUTH THAT IT WAS SO POOR THEY SCRAPPED IT?

Nina said very quietly: "Now we know it isn't a joke, don't we?"

CHAPTER ELEVEN

SURPRISING NEWS

A SUMMONS to the Head's study was most unusual.
Although Jill had no particular feeling of guilt her
heart did sink a trifle; but Miss Latimer, who'd given the
message to Jill and Nina, smiled slightly and said:
"Don't worry. It isn't a lecture."

On their way the two girls looked at each other blankly.

"Can't think what," Nina said.

"You don't suppose our missing sketch has fallen into
her hands?" Jill suggested.

Nina giggled. "You trying to sell me the idea she
pinched it?"

By the time they came to the door of the Head's study
they were absolutely solemn again. Jill knocked. The
door was opened by Miss Frant, who smiled cheerfully
and said: "Come in, girls."

Miss Manley was at her desk. She was a dignified
woman with a quiet voice and a very hard-wearing
brand of patience. She could look extremely severe and
was known to have silenced even sixth formers with a
solitary penetrating glance. But there was nothing
formidable in her manner as she greeted the girls and
told them to come nearer to her desk.

"Jill and Nina. I'll come to the point quickly. I
understand you've met a neighbour of ours—Miss
Garfield."

"Yes, Miss Manley," Jill said quickly. The thought
flashed into her mind that the walk had been unofficial,

taking place in what should have been a sports session. The best thing was to be frank about it. So she went on: "We should have been at tennis, only . . ."

The Head smiled. "Miss Frant has explained that. As there was no alternative programme you took exercise in the form of a walk and that's how you came to meet Miss Garfield, or rather one of her dogs."

"Yes, Miss Manley." Another uncomfortable thought presented itself to Jill. Perhaps the animal wasn't so well! Her voice faltered a little as she said: "I do hope the dog's none the worse. There was no antiseptic. Actually, when we got to the house I did suggest . . ."

"Quite unnecessary to go into all that," Miss Manley said quietly. She took up a letter. "I've received this from Miss Garfield. She mentions you both and says that if you're a fair sample of the girls of Hazelmere she must certainly reconsider her decision about the sports field. We may continue to rent it on the same terms as before."

Jill and Nina looked at each other in astonishment. They'd certainly never expected anything like this.

"Gosh! It's—it's wonderful!" Nina said excitedly.

"We didn't ask her," Jill said. "We wondered about it, but we felt it would be a mistake."

"I'm very sure you were right." There was a twinkle of amusement in the Head's clear grey eyes. "I think we can venture the opinion, with all respect, that Miss Garfield is inclined to be eccentric and that her reactions are unpredictable."

"She was a bit inclined to bully," Jill said diffidently. "No, not quite that. She gave commands and expected them to be obeyed—fast."

The Head smiled. "Having spoken to her, even though only over the telephone, I can well understand." She held herself a little more erect. "This is very good news for us, and I'm most pleased that your behaviour so impressed Miss Garfield. Jill and Nina—you've done very well for the school. And I'm sure the school will express its appreciation when Miss Frant gives the official news about the sports field. I thought you should be told in advance."

Jill and Nina left the Head's study with their minds in a whirl.

Nina said: "I never expected anything like that! I felt pretty embarrassed."

"So did I." Jill laughed. "We're not used to words of praise."

Nina gripped her hand. "This is about the best that could have happened. No! I'm not thinking of the whole school—just of the Fourth. Don't you see, Jill, this really puts you right on top as captain!"

"I suppose so. A few people like Ruth'll probably feel we've had all the luck."

"Luck!" Nina snorted. "Hey—what about our personal charm? We impressed Miss Garfield, didn't we?"

"I—honestly, pal, I still find it hard to believe. Trying to be fair, I suppose she must be very kind-hearted—deep down."

"Deep. You've said it! She hides that kind heart jolly well. If we'd displeased her in any way we'd have been tipped out in no time."

"I guess so." Jill thought for a minute. "I say—do we have to go and thank her? I reckon we should."

Nina put a hand to her head and gave a mock sigh. "Please, no problems! Let my poor brain get over the shock of all this, first."

"We might perhaps write a letter," Jill said thoughtfully.

They'd reached the common-room. Judy was curled up in a chair, frowning over a glossy magazine. She looked up as they entered, demanding: "What happened?"

"You'll learn, all in good time," Jill said.

Judy jumped up. "You can't keep it a secret! We all know the Head sent for you."

Muriel was among the other girls present. She said mournfully: "You might at least tell us whether you're being allowed to stay until the end of the term or leaving on the night train."

"Idiot!" Nina exploded.

"Well—called before the Head!" Muriel grimaced. "I should take my resignation with me."

"Stop fooling!" another girl shouted. "We want to know what happened."

Jill hesitated, finding it very awkward. They hadn't been asked to remain silent; but there was to be an official statement and they'd been told in advance.

Nina said: "If anyone's really bursting at the seams with curiosity, the best thing is to run along and ask Miss Frant."

"Was *she* there?" Judy gasped.

"She was," Nina affirmed.

"That doesn't sound like trouble," Muriel said. "I don't think she'd report anyone—not to the Head."

"Oh, you are exasperating!" Judy cried. "Well, you jolly well keep your rotten old secret." She flung herself down in the chair and renewed her study of her magazine.

"Hair," Muriel explained, pointing to the cover picture of a model's head.

"What about hair?" Nina asked.

"Judy doesn't know whether to have hers dyed a mouldy magenta or a putrid puce."

"I shall be thankful when I'm in the fifth form," Judy declared, trying to sound dignified. "The level of intelligence should be higher."

"She really *is* talking of having her hair tinted, and she'd get into awful trouble," one of the girls said seriously.

"Do shut up!" Judy exclaimed. "I'm not thinking of a very bright colour—and anyway, if I want advice I'll go to someone who really knows."

Jill looked at her watch. "Meanwhile it's time to look for food. And this afternoon there's tennis—we hope."

Muriel said: "There's a whisper Miss Frant locked old Mangold-wurzel in his potting shed just to make sure he didn't soak the courts again."

Nina lingered a little behind the others. Jill, understanding, waited for her. As soon as the corridor was clear, Nina rushed to the magazine box. It was empty.

Nina sighed. "Another blank. I don't want there to be anything. And yet I do. Do I sound crazy?"

Jill shook her head. "We'd both like the whole thing to fizzle out. Only we don't believe it will, so we want things to happen fast and get the miserable business settled."

"I wonder who's watching us and feeling a nasty, twisted satisfaction," Nina said thoughtfully.

Jill's hope for tennis that afternoon was fulfilled—but only partly. When she reached the courts she was confronted by an angry Vilma.

"You've turned up too late to help any!" Vilma snapped.

"What do you mean?" Jill remembered how important it was to keep the peace with Vilma and went on: "I'm five minutes late, I know; but it's not my fault. Miss Latimer caught me and was talking about restarting the debating society."

"Bother the debating society! Lindy's walked out on us."

This was a nasty shock. Jill had talked to Lindy, trying to be tactful with her, and had received a promise that the girl would do her best to get on form by practising hard. Lindy had stubbornly maintained, though, that she wouldn't be much good. "That's the way it is, Jill," she'd said. "I'm just not keen. I can't get with it. So how can I possibly play well?"

Now Jill looked thoughtfully at Vilma. "What happened? Lindy promised me she'd have a real go."

"She turned up. Actually, she came on court with me. She looked frightfully sulky about it, but she didn't argue. I asked her to serve first, and when she'd made two double faults, followed by a silly little pat-ball one that I simply tipped over the net out of her reach, I yelled to her to try serving with her eyes open. Well! She just threw down her racket and strode off!"

Jill groaned. Vilma had, of course, been tactless; but there was nothing to be gained by blaming her. Vilma was naturally impatient. She was a good captain and would keep her team up to scratch. But the team wouldn't have to resent her sharp comments.

Vilma said: "I called to her but she didn't answer." There was a dangerous flash in her eyes as she demanded: "Should I have gone running after her?"

Jill shook her head. She couldn't see Vilma doing any such thing; but even if she had it wouldn't have helped.

Vilma said: "I'd leave her to sulk for a while."

"She'll be in trouble—cutting practice. Her name's on the board as a member of the team. Miss Frant's sure

to spot that she's missing." Jill looked at her watch.
"I wonder if I can find Lindy in time."

"Huh! I wouldn't go to the trouble. But I don't think
you need worry about Miss Frant. She has a visitor.
That's why she's not here."

"Oh!" Jill was surprised.

"Games mistress from St. Hilda's. Remember what
their girls always say about her?"

"Non-stop talking."

"Yes. She was chattering away all the time they were
by the courts. Miss Frant escaped for a moment to tell
me to carry on, and then they went off—back to the
school."

"This was before the incident with Lindy?" Jill asked.

"Yes. Luckily for Lindy."

Jill thought for a moment or so. Then she said: "I'm
going after Lindy. Sorry, Vilma. It messes up team
practice, I know."

Vilma scowled. "Your decision. Will Nina go with
you?"

Jill hesitated. "Unless you want her."

Vilma shook her head. "I'm counting Lindy as being
right out. That means concentrating on Denise. You
and Nina will have to look after yourselves. You're not
the problem. According to my book you're a certain
winner. Nina has a fifty-fifty chance. And you should
just scrape through your doubles match."

"We'll try hard to do that little bit better," said
Jill.

"I'll improve Denise's play if it kills me—or her,"
Vilma said. Her temper was already subsiding.

Jill interrupted Nina, who was working on her backhand volleys, and explained what had happened. Together
they set off for the school buildings.

"Where do we look?" Nina asked. "The common-room. The dorm. A bit too obvious, I think. Vilma blows her top and then it's over; but Lindy's different. Get her in a bad mood and it sticks. She'll expect us to come looking for her and she'll be quite determined not to be hauled back to tennis."

"So?"

Nina pointed to the school gates.

"You could be right," Jill said slowly. "But if so she's really asking for trouble this time."

"We took a walk, remember."

"I know. But that afternoon the games had been cancelled with no alternative. Even so, we mightn't have got away with it so easily if it hadn't been for Miss Garfield."

"You're right," Nina said.

There was no such excuse for Lindy. If she'd left the school grounds she was playing truant just as much as if she'd dodged indoor lessons. She was running serious risks, too, because people might notice a solitary Hazelmere girl wandering around when it wasn't the half-day.

The more Jill thought about this, the gloomier she became. And Nina was just as unhappy. This was betrayed by her silence and her very solemn face. They didn't meet anyone at the school entrance but on the stairs they ran into Mary Curtis of the Fifth.

"Hallo. Not at tennis?"

"Had to come back for something," Jill explained, hoping Mary wouldn't ask further questions.

Mary patted Jill's shoulder. "I've just heard the great news about the sports field and the way you worked things with Miss Garfield. Super. Just super!"

"We had bags of luck," Jill said. "If it hadn't been

for a thorn and the fact that I can handle dogs, none of it would have happened."

Mary said: "There's a lot to be said for being in the right place at the right time." Her eyes twinkled. "Next meeting of the sports committee you'll probably receive an official vote of thanks, with only Hilda Wighton abstaining. Nothing personal, mind; just to be different from the Bish. Well, be seeing you."

Jill and Nina came to the top of the stairs and looked warily around. There was no one in the corridor and they rushed to the common-room. It was unoccupied.

"I thought she wouldn't be here," Jill said. "Have to check; but I'm sure you're right and she's on her way to town. Probably hopes to find one of her boy friends and pour out her troubles. Wonder if any of them will be sensible enough to give her some good advice."

"I doubt it," said Nina. "Where next?"

"The dorm. It's important to know if she's still in her tennis things."

Lindy wasn't. They saw her white skirt and her blazer immediately. They'd been flung on her bed. Socks and tennis pumps were on the floor.

Nina said: "I'll tidy this lot up. Anyone looking in here would notice these right away."

Jill, hardly listening, said: "She's left her blazer. So what's she wearing?"

"Worth checking," Nina replied.

So far as Jill could tell there were several clothing items missing. As she considered this she became increasingly uneasy.

"She wouldn't wear two grey skirts. Of course, one may have gone to be cleaned. I'm sure there are at least two cardigans missing. Her school hat's here, but her fancy scarf's gone." She went slowly to the locker beside

J.A.H.
D

Lindy's bed. Mentally apologising for this more personal prying, she turned the key and opened the door. Then she straightened up with a cry of dismay.

"Nina! This is quite empty! She's taken all her special possessions."

They stood looking at each other, their faces showing the alarm they felt. Then Jill flopped on the bed. "Oh, no? She can't have!"

"That's about it," Nina said. "She's run away from school." Her voice became urgent. "Jill! What the heck do we do now?"

CHAPTER TWELVE

CAUGHT!

THERE was a long silence in the dormitory. Jill slowly rose to her feet and went along to her own bed. Nina, watching her thoughtfully, said at last: "We go after her. Right?"

Jill shook her head. "*I* go after her."

Nina ran to her. "What on earth are you trying to say?"

"I'm talking sense, pal. Lindy must be brought back if it's possible. It could work out. If it doesn't . . ."

"She'll be in trouble and you'll be in trouble," Nina interrupted. "And you think I'll stay out of it? Well, think again!"

"Nina, be reasonable!"

Nina had already turned away. Hers was the next bed and she started to change out of her tennis clothes. Over her shoulder she said: " *Very* reasonable—that's me."

"No point in two of us . . ."

"Left to your own devices you'll land fair and square in a mess. Both your big feet right in it."

"My feet are not big!" Jill protested indignantly.

"You take a larger shoe than I do," Nina said triumphantly. She was more slender than Jill and had unusually small feet.

Jill, also changing, paused to observe: "Doesn't prove anything." She fastened her skirt, watching Nina out of the corner of her eyes.

Nina calmly went on with her dressing.

At last Jill exclaimed: "Look, I think you're being splendid; but it doesn't make sense. There's absolutely no point in *both* of us . . ."

"We're not sensible anyway," Nina said. "If we were, we'd do nothing about Lindy. She's being stupid and stupid people have to learn the hard way."

"She's stupid," Jill agreed. "But do you seriously suggest we should do nothing?"

Nina shook her head. "Of course not. We'll do everything else we can, including getting ourselves expelled." She sighed. "I just wish it could be in a better cause."

Jill tried once again to dissuade Nina, but secretly she knew it was useless. Finally she gave in. "But as form captain I think you should have obeyed me." She gave Nina's arm an affectionate squeeze. "Might as well argue with a brick wall."

"That's been said to me before," Nina murmured. "Can't think who. Or why."

They left the dormitory and came to the top of the stairs. Jill peered over.

"Coast's clear," she said.

They hurried down. When they reached the corridor they heard steps and dived into the shelter of the common-room. Jill stood by the door, listening. The steps came nearer, passed them, and faded.

"Probably matron," Jill said. "Ready?"

They stepped out cautiously. Jill kept telling herself that so far they weren't running any great risk. The only danger lay in someone in authority noticing them and at the same time realising they should be dressed for tennis. So the chances of getting to the gates without being stopped were fairly good. It seemed reassuring, but her tension was still there.

They hurried downstairs and across the wide entrance hall.

"Coats?" Nina suggested.

"No. Going like this we're not too obviously Hazelmere girls."

They were wearing grey skirts and cardigans and had already decided not to wear hats. Lindy had done much the same, but she had the additional advantage after passing through the gates, Jill decided, of wearing a headscarf and using make-up which would make her look older.

Nina said: "Suppose we run into someone who does ask questions. What do we say?"

"As little as possible." Jill was looking in all directions.

"I think we're in luck. Make for the walnut tree first and then cut across."

"We could be seen from the offices," Nina warned.

"That's only a risk if the Head happens to be there."

"Golly! It's terribly easy to imagine I can see her at the window!"

Jill was more nervous about the last few yards and she breathed comparatively easily when they were through the gates and hurrying along the road. A little breathless they reached the bus stop. Jill looked at her watch.

"If the bus is on time we've only a couple of minutes to wait."

"And where do we go? Have you thought of that?" Nina asked. "She's a choice of long-distance bus or train."

Jill had been working this out. If Lindy had decided on going by bus, they'd have no chance of catching up with her. She could, at the main bus stop, have taken any of a number of buses. On the other hand the station, as a waiting place, was less conspicuous, so there seemed a good chance this would be Lindy's choice. Anyway, it was their only hope. And Jill happened to know that the bus on which she and Nina would be travelling would reach the railway station in time to connect with the one afternoon through train.

She explained her reasoning and Nina agreed their best bet was to try the station.

"D'you think she'll make for home?" Jill asked.

Nina frowned. "I don't know. She doesn't talk much about her people. I've heard her say that her father spends a lot of time on the Continent—he's in some sort of export business. And her mother sometimes closes up the house. If there's no one at home and Lindy can get in, she'll be safe in a way, I suppose. But there's food to buy and . . ."

Nina paused, suddenly appalled by the prospect in front of Lindy if they didn't catch her in time.

"I've an idea there's an aunt who's always been very kind to her and who lives near her home. She might go there."

The bus arrived. Nina said: "Just our luck if one of the mistresses steps down from it."

"You're about as discouraging as Muriel."

"Sorry." Nina sighed. "I guess the thought of Lindy has a depressing effect."

Nina's immediate fears were groundless. No one alighted from the bus. The two girls went right to the back. They tried to appear at ease, but they had a few bad moments when the conductor took their fares. He was so slow in giving the tickets that they feared he was suspicious. It was only afterwards that they realised he must be new to the job and was taking great care to issue correct tickets.

Nina said quietly: "Suppose we catch Lindy. Thought how we cope with her?"

"Just hoping she'll listen to some common sense. She's not too bad, you know, really. The thought that we're taking chances for her will register."

"I hope it does," Nina said. "So far Lindy's done too much thinking about Lindy."

To the girls, anxious and tensed, it seemed no bus had ever been slower. What calmness they were able to muster nearly collapsed when a traffic hold-up stopped the bus for about five minutes. A minor accident had caused a lorry to completely block the roadway of a narrow street on the outskirts of the town.

Nina, her hands tightly clasped, muttered: "Oh, come on! Come on!"

At last the traffic was on the move again. Jill looked at her watch. "If I'm right about the train-time we'll still have a few minutes in hand."

"We'll need them, searching for Lindy."

"She'll keep out of sight. Ladies' waiting-room, I guess. She might risk the buffet. I don't know."

The bus finally turned in at the station entrance. Jill and Nina hurriedly bought platform tickets. The ticket collector, talking to one of the porters, scarcely noticed the two girls.

"Well, we've got here safely," said Jill, sighing her relief.

Nina was already looking along the platform. Not many people were waiting. A few were grouped near the bookstall. Lindy was not among them. Neither was she at the small kiosk where sweets and fruit were sold.

"The waiting-room," Jill said.

A minute later they were gazing at each other in dejection. Nina said, in a small voice: "We're wrong. She's not going by train."

Very slowly they turned and went out to the platform again. Jill felt thoroughly down-hearted; but at the same time she stubbornly refused to accept defeat.

"She *must* be intending to catch this next train," she said. "It makes sense—at least, as much sense as there can be in anything so stupid as she's doing."

"It's possible she's afraid she'll be followed," Nina suggested, "and is leaving coming on to the station as long as she can. There are two tatty-looking cafés opposite. She may be in one of those."

"Cutting it fine." Jill glanced at the station clock. "The train will be signalled any minute now. Oh! I wish we could inquire at the booking office. Daren't though—no knowing what we might start."

As they looked despairingly up and down the platform there was a clatter and the signal arm jerked down. And at this moment Nina noticed a furtive movement. She gripped Jill's arm.

"Down there—the telephone box."

"You certain?"

"Not absolutely," Nina confessed. "Whoever's there

stepped out and then back again. I don't think she looked our way."

"Come on," Jill said. "But nothing rash. If we pounce on the wrong person we'll probably finish up in a police cell!"

They moved unhurriedly, keeping close to the station buildings so that whoever was just the other side of the phone box shouldn't see them.

"If it's Lindy," Jill said, " she'll be watching the platform entrance. Then if anyone she knows comes into sight, she'll nip into the box and keep her back turned."

"Bet she was in there when we came along the platform."

"Mmm. If you remember, there was a porter wheeling a stack of luggage. He was between us and the phone box—so there's a chance that as we didn't see her, she didn't see us either."

They came to the box. Jill edged round it just at the moment the train roared into the station. There was a flurried movement of people. The girl behind the telephone box stepped out, rather furtively, head lowered. And Jill darted to her.

The girl was Lindy. She gave a stifled scream and gasped: "Jill! What are you doing here?"

"Saving you from making a complete mess of things."

"You mustn't stop me, Jill! I must go. Honest, I . . ."

Nina took Lindy's arm. "You don't want to have a scene right here, do you? We'll stop you from going on this train—but it's likely to start a horrid fuss."

For a moment it seemed Lindy would try to struggle past them and make a dash for it. But the compartment doors were already slamming. She turned an agonised face to Jill. "Why did you do it? Why didn't you leave me alone?"

Jill was trying hard to think of the right things to say. "Come on, Lindy. You're all upset about things and you won't make them any easier by running away. It won't work. Come on—let's get back to school."

The train was pulling out. There was a delay when they reached the ticket collector. He said that Lindy might be able to get a refund as she hadn't used her ticket; but the girls thanked him for his advice and then cleared off as fast as they could.

"Start claiming a refund and we might be there for ages," Jill said.

"You're lucky to have the chance of losing no more than a railway fare," Nina commented, unusually severely for her.

Lindy didn't answer. From the moment the train had started to move off her mood had changed. She was now so apathetic that Jill was a little worried about her.

"Are you all right, Lindy?"

Lindy nodded but said nothing.

"I know the best thing would be to go somewhere and have a cup of tea; but we can't risk it. We've all been away from school quite long enough."

Lindy stared at Jill, and then at Nina. "Gosh! I hadn't thought about you two. Not properly, I mean. You're likely to be in trouble yourselves."

"Let's hope we can sneak in without being spotted," Jill said.

"You shouldn't have done it. You should've let me go. It doesn't matter what happens to me, but you're different."

"And you're talking nonsense." Jill spoke sharply. "You matter as much as anyone else."

Fortunately they didn't have to wait long for a bus. It was a very silent journey back to the school. Lindy sat with her head lowered, Nina was thoughtful, and Jill kept looking at her watch and wishing the bus would go faster.

At last they reached the stop near the school. Jill, checking on the time once more, said: "I think we'll have to leave Lindy's case in the bushes by the side gate. There'll be too many people about right now. Then we'll sneak past the office block and make it seem that we've just been strolling and chatting. Take that head-scarf off, Lindy."

Lindy obeyed and they hurried towards the gates.

"I'm getting dithery," Nina said.

"Nearly there," Jill encouraged. Then she stopped with a low cry of dismay. A girl had stepped out from the school gates and was looking straight at them.

"Hilda Wighton!" Nina exclaimed in horror.

The prefect started to walk towards them. Jill groaned. It was bitter to be caught just on the last few yards—but caught they were and there'd be no way out of it.

CHAPTER THIRTEEN

WHO TOLD?

"THREE of you!" Hilda Wighton exclaimed. "I don't have to ask where you've been. I know, because I saw you step down from the bus." Her rather pale face was uncompromisingly stern and Jill knew immediately that it would be useless making any sort of appeal to her.

The prefect had noticed the case Lindy was carrying. She indicated it and said: "That is yours?"

After the slightest hesitation Lindy murmured: "Yes, it's mine."

"Did you have permission to go into town?" Hilda Wighton demanded.

"I'm afraid not," Jill said. She realised to the full that they were in a very nasty position. There was nothing to be gained by giving evasive answers or trying to make excuses.

"This is too serious for me to deal with as a prefect," Hilda Wighton said. "You're fourth form. I could take you straight to the Head, but I think the fairest thing is to report you to your form mistress. You'd better follow me." She swung round and walked briskly towards the school.

Nina gave a low groan and whispered: "It would be Hilda Wighton! If the Bish had caught us there might have been a chance."

"I doubt it," Jill said.

Lindy said shakily: "I've let you in for this. If you hadn't come after me. . . . Though it proves you'd have done better to leave me alone. All the same, I'm sorry."

"Thanks," Nina murmured. "Afraid I don't see how your sorrow's going to help us, though."

There were a few girls around and some curious eyes were watching the three fourth formers as they followed the prefect into the building.

"It'll be all over school in no time," Jill whispered.

Hilda Wighton led them to the fourth form classroom. "You wait here," she said. "I'm going along to the mistresses' common-room." She closed the door behind her with ominous care.

"Now for it," Nina said. "I wonder what'll happen.

I suppose Hilda Wighton takes us to Miss Latimer, and Miss Latimer takes us to the Head." She grimaced. "Somehow I don't think it'll be anywhere near as pleasant as the last time we were in her study."

"We can only wait and see," Jill said gloomily.

Lindy moaned: "Oh, I do wish you two hadn't got mixed up in all this. It's all my fault. I . . ."

"Do be sensible, Lindy," Nina said sharply. "You're in a bigger mess than we are, I'd say. Your best chance is to try to explain to Miss Latimer. She may at least be sympathetic. And just leave us to look after our own worries."

"I wish we'd had more experience of Miss Latimer," Jill said. "She doesn't seem too bad, but there hasn't been time to get to know her properly. She takes things quietly and doesn't get mad. But is it that she's a bit reserved, or is she a bit icy?"

Nina sighed. "I'm afraid we're going to learn the answer very quickly."

There was a heavy silence in the classroom. Then there were quick steps along the corridor and the door was opened. Miss Latimer came in, followed by Hilda Wighton. The prefect looked more severe than the mistress, who approached the girls slowly, her expression thoughtful.

Miss Latimer glanced back at the door. "That will be all, thank you, Hilda."

It wasn't possible to tell whether the prefect was relieved or disappointed. She said: "Very well, Miss Latimer," and went out.

Everything depended on Miss Latimer now. She was a fairly young mistress, still in her twenties. She always gave the appearance of being unruffled, her very clear grey eyes having some part in this.

Her voice was almost reassuringly calm when she said: "Which one of you is going to tell me what all this is about?"

There was an awkward pause. Jill tried desperately hard to think what she could say without immediately dragging Lindy's name into the story. She began: "I was a little late getting down to the courts for tennis, Miss Latimer."

The mistress nodded. "Yes. I was responsible for that. I didn't realise the time when I stopped you. So—you reached the tennis courts. What happened next?"

While Jill was hesitating Lindy suddenly exclaimed: "It was all my fault! I'm the only one to blame, Miss Latimer. Jill and Nina only came after me because I was running away!"

Miss Latimer looked surprised, but only for a moment. "So that's the meaning of the suitcase," she said.

Lindy's head was lowered. Unexpectedly she started to sob bitterly.

Miss Latimer said: "Now don't get too upset, Lindy. We'll have a quiet talk." She turned to Jill and Nina. "Perhaps you should have told someone what you were doing—though I do realise the difficulty. I'll see you later; but don't worry about that. Take Lindy's case up to the dormitory, will you?"

"Yes, of course. Thank you, Miss Latimer."

Jill and Nina hurried away. As they reached the stairs they looked back and saw Miss Latimer coming away from the classroom. She had Lindy with her and her hand was on the girl's shoulder.

Jill said softly: "I think Lindy's going to be all right."

Nina nodded. "Yes. In her quiet way I think Miss Latimer's expert at coping with situations. But can she deal with this one without going to the Head?"

"Don't ask me. All I know is we seem to be forgiven. She *did* say not to worry, didn't she?"

"And she understood it would have been difficult for us to tell anyone what we were doing. That shook me!"

In the dormitory they placed Lindy's case by the side of her bed. "I wonder why she tried to clear out," Jill said thoughtfully. "Being generally fed up—that's not strong enough, surely? Vilma exploding at her. . . ."

"Might have been the last straw. But in itself it's nothing—specially as Vilma's always exploding."

As they started to leave the dormitory Jill said: "Oh! Why try to work it out? It's Lindy's affair. Perhaps we'll never know the answer. I just hope she tells Miss Latimer everything; that's all."

Near the top of the stairs Nina stopped. "Jill, before we go to the common-room and get masses of questions shot at us . . ."

"Yes? What?"

"Something's worrying me."

"Give," Jill encouraged.

"Remember what Hilda Wighton said when she came face to face with us?"

Jill frowned. "You tell me."

"I'm sure of this, Jill. She said: ' Three of you! ' and sounded surprised. As if she'd expected some, but not three. Perhaps two."

Jill stared at Nina. "What are you getting at?"

"She was waiting for the bus, wasn't she? On the lookout. She actually saw us get off. Now why? How did she know? My guess is that somebody told her Jill Rodgers and Nina Cassel had sneaked off and gone into town. But the sixty-four thousand dollar question is—who told?"

Jill was shocked. "It's hard to believe!"

They stood on the landing for a minute or so, silent, looking at each other, their faces troubled.

It was not until after prep that Miss Latimer had the promised word with Jill and Nina. The fourth form had been buzzing with rumours and the two friends had been bombarded with questions. They'd said very little, to the exasperation of those who were eager for news. Lindy didn't show up and nobody knew what had happened to her.

Right at the end of prep Miss Latimer, who'd been taking the period, asked the two girls to remain and told the others to go. There were whispers and a lot of backward glances, but at last the room was empty except for Miss Latimer, Jill, and Nina.

The girls went forward to her desk. Miss Latimer came round and leaned back against it in a casual way that clearly indicated this was to be a friendly talk.

The mistress said: "I suppose you didn't know for certain that Lindy would be trying to catch the afternoon train?"

"It was a guess, Miss Latimer," Jill replied. "At least, it seemed to me the most likely thing she'd do."

"You were very bright; and I'm thankful you were there in time to stop her from doing something extremely foolish. It might not have turned out so well, though."

"We were lucky," Jill agreed.

"I'm glad you realise that. It may help you to see you *should* have told someone as soon as you'd reason to suspect Lindy was running away from school." She went on quickly: "Yes, I know. It would seem like tale-bearing and we rather shrink from that sort of thing, don't we? But there are times when it's justified. And this was one of them. If you hadn't found Lindy it would have meant that any official search for her would have started later than was necessary. And the longer a search is delayed the more difficult it becomes."

"I'm sorry, Miss Latimer," Jill said. "We just didn't think of that."

"We were awfully anxious to bring Lindy back as quickly as possible," Nina said eagerly.

Miss Latimer nodded. "That's what I've assured the Head. Yes, I had to tell her what had happened." Unexpectedly she smiled. "So you see I know from experience that one sometimes has to do the uncomfortable thing—like telling tales." She became serious again. "The Head does feel that although you were a little rash, you did your best. So you'll hear no more of this."

"Thank you, Miss Latimer!" Jill said fervently.

"We're very grateful that you put in a word for us," Nina said.

Miss Latimer continued: "Now I want to ask you about Lindy. Has she talked much to you?"

"Very little," Jill said. "She's sometimes said that she's fed up with school, but that's about all."

"Has she confided in anyone?"

"I don't think so, Miss Latimer." Nina answered, this time.

"She's no special friends then?"

Nina explained that Lindy had been most friendly with Pam Ralston, the previous captain of the Fourth, who'd now left Hazelmere. "Nobody's taken Pam's place with her," she concluded.

"Lindy's not been cold-shouldered," Jill hastened to say. "It's just that she's not wanted to join in. There's a place for her in the tennis team; she's been selected. But she's not keen. She's been asked to help with the concert, but she doesn't want to do anything."

Miss Latimer said: "Perhaps things'll be a bit better now. I want you to be patient, Jill, as form captain. You can't expect Lindy to suddenly change and become all enthusiasm."

"We're very willing to help all we can," Jill promised.

"I'm sure of that. I shall rely on you." And Miss Latimer turned away.

Jill hesitated before saying: "Please, Miss Latimer, what's happened to Lindy?"

"If you mean punishment—nothing's happened," Miss Latimer said quietly. She, too, hesitated for a moment. "You know, when people brood over their troubles, getting all steamed up inside, they often make wrong decisions and do something foolish. But it's not very sensible to punish them if it can possibly be avoided. Much better to iron out the troubles. Lindy's unburdened herself but she found it something of a strain; so the Head decided she should spend the evening with matron."

"Thank you for telling us, Miss Latimer," Jill said.

"That's all, girls. Good night." Miss Latimer began to gather up some exercise books she had been correcting.

Jill and Nina felt much easier in mind as they made their way to the common-room. Nina remarked that one good thing to come out of the affair was their better understanding of Miss Latimer.

"She's super!" Jill said with enthusiasm.

"The best form mistress in the school, maybe," Nina suggested.

"Why not? The best form, after all."

"In most ways," Nina said.

Jill sighed, knowing what Nina was thinking. Somebody had warned Hilda Wighton that they'd left the school grounds. Who? One of their own form mates?

Who else could it be? And yet . . . "If only we could ask Hilda who split on us!" she burst out.

"Ask Hilda! Gosh! She certainly wouldn't tell us, and very likely she *would* report us for insolence." Nina went on thoughtfully: "But it's terribly important. Unless I'm way off the beam whoever told about us this afternoon is the same person as the sender of the nasty anonymous notes! They do go together, don't they?"

CHAPTER FOURTEEN

ABOUT LINDY

THAT night Jill was actually glad when bedtime came. A garbled version of Lindy's doings had spread like wildfire, and both Jill and Nina grew tired of contradicting it. They were careful not to say a word more than was necessary, and this didn't suit some of their questioners who responded by demanding more and more answers.

Nina had eventually flared: "What do you expect? A special edition of the fourth form mag with the full story on the front page?"

It was so unusual for Nina to display temper that the other girls were silenced and this gave Jill a chance to suggest it was high time they changed the subject.

There was another topic of great interest, because the news that Long Field would still be rented by the school had been whispered around for a few hours and was confirmed by an official statement appearing on each notice board. Jill and Nina happened to be standing near one of these when Ann Page had appeared with the typed sheets and pinned one up. She completely ignored the two girls.

Sitting on the edge of Jill's bed after lights out, Nina remembered this and said: "I just don't get Ann Page. Why the nose-in-the-air act?"

"Forget her. I couldn't care less." Jill frowned. "There are far more worrying things."

"You don't have to tell me that. Those unsigned messages addressed to the editor. All my typing work on our sketch."

Jill was only half listening. Who'd sent the anonymous notes? The same person who'd gone tale-bearing to Hilda Wighton?

Jill still found it terribly hard to believe anyone in the Fourth capable of such meanness.

Nina said: "Don't let it get you down. Things'll work out, given time."

"Huh! Time! What about the sketch? We need it. Have you thought of anything we can do?"

"I wish I could be *sure* what's best. One thing—we could report the folder as missing. Not blaming anyone, of course."

"Report it to Miss Latimer, you mean?"

"Who else? She's form mistress. And she's certainly shown to-day that she'll do what she can to help when things go wrong."

"She was wonderful. But that's one reason why I'd hate to bother her about anything else right now."

"You've a point there," Nina agreed.

There was a slight sound at the end of the dormitory and both girls looked round sharply. A shadowy figure holding a small torch came forward hesitantly and then, when one of the other girls spoke to her, rushed along the dormitory to Jill's bed. It was Lindy.

"'Lo there," Jill said. She twisted round, punched her pillow and sat up higher. "Sit down. Make yourself comfortable and if there isn't enough space just shove me out. Nina does."

"I do not!" Nina exclaimed with mock indignation. "If ever you fall out it's your own silly fault for pretending you're go-kart racing."

This exchange had the desired effect of putting Lindy more at ease. Judy slipped from her bed and came scurrying across. Nina jumped up, intercepted her, and hissed fiercely: "Beat it!" Judy scuttled back to bed.

Lindy said in a very subdued voice: "I want to thank you for all you did."

"Forget it," Jill said. "We didn't do too well, you know. Walking into Hilda Wighton of all people! That moment's going to haunt me."

"It wasn't your fault. I was awfully glad when Miss Latimer told me you weren't going to be hauled up in front of the Head—not that she put it like that, of course."

"Was the Head terrifyingly fierce?" Nina asked.

"No. She was very kind. I think I've Miss Latimer to thank for that. You know, sort of explaining things for me."

Jill wanted to ask what things; but she didn't wish to pry. There was a pause which threatened to become awkward. Then Nina said: "Well, it's not finished up too badly, has it?"

"I don't know how it'll work out," Lindy said. "I mean, things couldn't be settled right away."

Jill shook her head. "Don't get it," she protested.

"I'm telling you awfully badly. I *want* to explain, but it's difficult." Lindy paused for a moment, then went on: "I've been absolutely miserable. All this term,

I mean. You see things weren't too good at home last hols. My father was away on business. All the time. I never saw him. Then Mother was off on one thing and another. She's pretty clever, you know, and she's in partnership with a friend in an antiques business. Mother does most of the buying, so she's off here there and everywhere to sales."

"Not much of a holiday for you," Jill murmured.

"It was so boring," Lindy said. "I was on my own nearly all the time—except for Mrs. Tate, that is. She cleans the place and cooks meals, and Mother got her to stay at nights when she herself was away. But I might just as well have been on my own."

"But surely your mother had a few days—when the shop was closed, for instance," Nina suggested.

Lindy shook her head. "Mother was showing a special client—a wealthy American woman—around the West country. Acting as a sort of guide and getting some business."

Jill said: "I'd have thought that would make you glad to get back to school."

"Why? It might have done if Pam was still here—but she's gone. And what is there at the end of the term? The next hols will be just like the last. It's somehow so hopeless, so dull and futile. I feel as if my life's all tied up. And until to-day I could only see one way out—escape from school and start living on my own. Pretend to be older and find a job."

"You'd never get away with that!" Jill exclaimed.

"I suppose not." Lindy sighed. "You know, I get letters from Pam. She's having a super time. But then, her people are grand. I went there once, for a fortnight. I'll never forget it."

"Well, go to bed now and don't let yourself think about

anything else until you go to sleep," said Jill with a flash
of inspiration. "Just try to remember every little thing
that made it a wonderful holiday—then perhaps you'll
dream about it and wake up in the morning feeling ever
so much better."

"You'll have lots more happy memories from now on,"
Nina encouraged. "We'll help. And it looks like the
Head and Miss Latimer will do what they can, too. Slip
into bed as fast as you can—and good luck for the future!"

Lindy stood up. She hesitated and then said: "Thank
you—both of you—for everything." Then she turned
quickly and hurried to her bed.

"Poor kid," Nina whispered. "If I'd known she was
really unhappy I wouldn't have been so annoyed with
her. I wonder what the Head'll do; seems she has some
ideas."

"We can't just leave it to the Head, though," said
Jill. "We'll have to do whatever we can."

Jill found herself involved in Lindy's affairs the very
next day. Passing the fourth form notice board her eye
was caught by alterations to the tennis list. Lindy's
name had been crossed out. Denise Trent had been
moved up from reserve player and the new reserve was
Muriel Davis.

Jill went in search of Vilma Blake and finally discovered
her in the library.

"I was looking for you earlier," Vilma said. "They
told me you'd been called to a sports committee meeting."

Jill nodded. "Only a short one. Just to change some
plans now we still have Long Field." She paused. "I've
seen the tennis list, Vilma."

"You weren't around so I made the necessary changes.
If you'd been there I'd have told you first."

Jill wished she had been consulted. In fairness, Vilma was within her rights. Perhaps lacking a little in courtesy; but Jill decided to overlook this. She said: "I rather wish you hadn't been in such a hurry."

There was a challenging look from Vilma, who never took kindly to the merest hint of criticism. "Why?"

"Well, you've dropped Lindy."

"Why not? What about her performance yesterday? Anyway, I don't know that I've dropped her. She dropped herself."

Jill said: "She's been having rather a bad time—some sort of home problems. They're being sorted out now."

Vilma said: "There's nothing personal in this; it's not dislike of Lindy. We want the best team if we're to beat St. Hilda's. Lindy's off form, out of practice—*and* suffering from temperament. She's a dead loss."

"There's time for her to get back on form," Jill urged. She noticed the little indications that Vilma's temper was likely to flare; a raising of the head, eyebrows almost meeting in a frown, eyes seeming to sparkle. So she went on quickly but quietly: "It's not as though she's being replaced by a player who's almost as good. Even when she's off form Lindy could beat Denise, though not so easily."

"And what about her tantrums?" Vilma demanded. "I can see her throwing down her racket on the big day. We'd lose the match and, worse still, have the whole of St. Hilda's sniggering at us."

Jill shook her head emphatically. "It won't happen," she promised. "I wish you'd give Lindy another chance, Vilma. It could mean a lot to her."

"And this means a lot to me," Vilma said sharply. "You didn't have to make me captain of the tennis team. But while I am, I'm going to *be* captain. I said Lindy's out—and so she is. You put her back—and I walk out."

The two girls stared hard at each other. This was their first open clash. Jill did some fast thinking. The good of the school had to come first and Vilma was their strongest player. With her, they should be able to win, even with a weaker player like Denise in their side. Without her, defeat would be virtually a certainty. Jill took a deep breath and accepted defeat. "I'm sorry you don't feel you can go back on the changes you've made, but it's your decision, Vilma."

Vilma looked rather surprised; then, as Jill turned away, she said: "I'm glad it didn't come to a quarrel, Jill."

"Is that due to you—or to me?" Jill asked. She didn't wait for an answer, but left the library and went along to the common-room. Nina was waiting for her by arrangement.

Nina looked across and said: "It didn't go too well."

"It certainly didn't. She threatened a walk-out. What could I do?"

Nina said: "What you did do. The sensible thing. Don't worry about it. It's not a tragedy."

"I want to help Lindy."

"Of course. But Lindy's not going to get into a state over being dropped from the tennis team. She may be sorry later on; but right now she couldn't care less."

"Where is she?" Jill asked.

"Under one of the walnut trees. I invited her to come for a walk with us as it's a free afternoon. Honestly, I was scared she might push off to town again and get herself all mixed up once more."

"Okay," Jill approved. "Where do we go?"

"Where can we go? There's not much left. Just the common. We could play ring o' roses, or something."

As they left the common-room Nina glanced at the magazine box and shook her head. "Miss Anonymous seems to have slipped up. I was certain she'd have something to say about yesterday's events."

"If I'm really her target she's probably feeling a bit down-hearted. Not expelled. Still captain of the form. Not even gated."

Nina laughed. "That's the way to treat it!"

"I wish we could, all the time, think of it that way. But it's so thoroughly nasty it seems almost evil."

Nina wasn't laughing now. "I know. And what really worries me is that there's more to it than the messages. Our play disappears. Somebody tells tales when we go after Lindy. What happens next? Something will!"

"You're a real comfort," Jill said.

"I'm just trying to warn you. Watch how you go. It applies to me, too, and I'm jolly well keeping my eyes open all the time."

They came down the stone steps from the school and went across to the bench where Lindy was waiting.

"It's good of you . . ." Lindy began.

Jill interrupted. "Afraid it's not going to be very exciting."

"I don't want that," Lindy said slowly. "I want to be some place that's quiet and not crowded. It's been rotten this morning—feeling everyone staring at me and whispering behind my back."

"Come off it!" Jill said quickly. "I know there's some curiosity, but not nearly so much as you think. You're just imagining."

"Perhaps I am," said Lindy, glancing back at the school. "But imagining or not, I'm glad to be getting away for a little while."

They walked on, none of them saying much, until they

were crossing the short grass between the bushes. Then Lindy said. "There's something I want to say, Jill."

"Go ahead," Jill encouraged.

"I see Vilma's cut me out of the tennis team."

"Oh, that," said Jill, grimacing.

"Not to worry. Listen, Jill, I don't want you to fall out with Vilma over it."

"How do you know she did it off her own bat?"

"I heard Ruth saying so, and she said it would be interesting to see if there was a show-down over it."

Jill drew a deep breath. "Ruth!"

"She didn't realise I was behind her and near enough to hear. Well, I wouldn't like that to happen over me."

"Don't lose any sleep," Jill said with a wry smile. "I did ask Vilma to think again, but there was nothing doing. Sorry I couldn't insist; but there was rather a lot to consider."

"Oh, I do understand," Lindy said. "I wouldn't be happy trying to play for Vilma, anyway. I'd feel she was—you know, watching every movement. Besides, I'm off form."

"Some hard practice would put that right."

"I don't think I'm running round in small circles now; I can't settle down yet." Lindy hesitated. "I hope I'll be able to. Last night I thought things were going to be different; but this morning it looked exactly the same old world."

"Give it time. Not that the world's going to change. But you'll see it differently."

"That sounds very wise," Lindy said, managing a small smile.

"If so I must've got it out of a book."

Nina, a little ahead of them, stopped at a fallen tree.

She sat down, calling over her shoulder: "If you want to be energetic don't mind me."

Jill and Lindy joined her. They sat for a time, talking. Jill found it rather difficult, because certain subjects had to be avoided. Tennis. And the concert, at which Lindy had refused to sing.

The sun was very hot and at last Nina said: "Why not find some shade? I'm roasting."

We can go to the edge of the wood," Jill suggested. "The trees overhang the fence a bit here and there."

They were very close to this when Lindy suddenly pointed. "Look!"

Jill had a swift impression of green and yellow, then the bird was hidden.

"Green woodpecker," Lindy said.

They moved cautiously, peering up, but the bird had disappeared. Perhaps it knew and was mocking them when it called "Ha-ha-ha."

"Hey! Girls!"

It was a loud shout and it startled them. They turned quickly and Nina exclaimed: "It's Miss Garfield—by the gate. And she seems to be beckoning to us."

Jill said: "Gosh! We haven't written to her yet. I did try, but I couldn't think what to say."

As soon as they were near the gate Miss Garfield started to talk in a very loud voice. "Stood here and waved to you. Might as well have signalled three statues. Called and you were stone deaf!"

"Sorry, Miss Garfield," Jill said, anxious to appease her. Miss Garfield was very important to the school and mustn't be upset.

Ignoring this, Miss Garfield demanded: "What were you gawping up at?"

"Lindy saw a green woodpecker. Oh, this is Lindy

Sinclair, Miss Garfield." Jill remembered the introduction just in time.

"Male or female?" Miss Garfield demanded.

For a moment Jill was disconcerted; then she realised Miss Garfield was talking about the woodpecker. Jill looked helplessly at Lindy.

"They're not easy to tell," Lindy said.

Miss Garfield nodded. "Green woodpecker. I must remember. You good at bird spotting?"

Nina volunteered: "Lindy's the best in our form. We've all done a little. We used to . . ." She stopped, a little disconcerted.

"Come into these woods, I suppose you mean?"

There was a hint of aggression and Jill said firmly: "We had permission, of course."

"Oh, you did!" Miss Garfield almost glared at Jill, who faced her unflinchingly, feeling this was a point which must be established fairly and squarely no matter what. Suddenly, still looking quite fierce, Miss Garfield said: "So you can identify wild birds and you know your way around the woods. Then you can get to work. Come along!"

"Work!" Jill gasped. "What sort of work?"

"Have you forgotten my friend who takes wildlife films? Coming down next month, and I'm expected to make a list of what kinds of birds I've got in these woods." With a sudden friendly grin she added: "*Me!* . . . Well, I love birds, but I can never remember what they're called; so how can I make a list? Most of 'em have got silly names, anyway. Green woodpecker, for instance. He's as much yellow as green. I do know that much. Oh, come on! Get busy! Find some birds, jot down their names, and tell me at tea-time. There should be some cake. Now what else was I going to do besides look

for birds? Oh, I know. I've lost Barney—he tore off
after an imaginary hare." She hurried away, calling,
"Barney!" as loudly as she could every few moments.

Nina gurgling with laughter gasped: "Making all
that noise she'll scare off every bird within ten miles."

Lindy, very bewildered, said: "What an extraordinary
woman. And what's just as extraordinary, I think I like
her. Mmm. Like her lots."

CHAPTER FIFTEEN

A CLUE AT LAST

ON THEIR way back to the school Nina said: "She really
is a crazy one!"

The tea party had been very much like the first one,
with Miss Garfield grumbling at and about Gertrude,
while the parrot enlivened the scene by screeching rude
remarks.

"She's a pet," Lindy said.

"You certainly seemed to get on very well with her,"
Jill commented. "Better, I think, than Nina and I. What
was she talking about when she dragged you off into the
conservatory? We could see you both jabbering away
like mad."

"Oh, she was awfully nice. She doesn't miss much,
you know. She said quite bluntly that she could see I'm
not so happy as my two friends, and she asked me why.
I didn't tell her everything, of course; but she seemed to
understand. She actually ran away from school, herself,
she told me."

Nina smiled mischieveously. "That's amazing! Now

I'd have expected the school, mistresses and all, to run away from *her*—hard and fast!"

Lindy laughed. "She doesn't mean any of the dreadful things she says. You realise that, surely?"

"We do," Jill told her.

Lindy hesitated. "Look—I hope you don't mind. She invited me to tea on Sunday!"

Jill was surprised. So was Nina, who exclaimed: "You were getting on even better together than I thought!"

"Why should we mind?" Jill asked. "I'm very glad to hear it, Lindy."

"So'm I," Nina assured her. "No reason you should feel bad about it. She doesn't belong to us." Her eyes twinkled. "I'm glad she doesn't. I think we'd find her a bit of a responsibility. I'm all for a simple, uncomplicated life!"

"She's turning one of the greenhouses into an aviary," Lindy explained. "And someone's coming over on Sunday to deliver—oh, I don't know how many budgies. She thought I'd like to help her introduce them to their new quarters. At least, that's the way she put it."

"Super!" Jill cried. "You'll love that."

"It was very kind of her," Lindy said. "But when I told her so, she covered it up by saying that if I came along Gertrude would be sure to make a cake. She tries to avoid it normally, because she thinks Miss Garfield should diet and cake's fattening."

"And Miss Garfield doesn't like the idea of dieting," Nina murmured. "I bet that was genuine enough, Lindy."

By this time they were approaching the wide steps of the main entrance to the school building. Vilma Blake was a little ahead of them. She paused and waited.

"Oh, Jill. I've just been getting together the typed copy of our sketch." Vilma's manner was friendly and it seemed the tennis team incident was forgotten.

Jill glanced at the papers Vilma was holding. "Good," she said. "Are you pleased with it?"

"Reasonably. I'm wondering about taking it to Miss Latimer. Has yours gone to her yet?"

Jill shook her head.

"When are you handing it in, then?"

It was the question Jill had been hoping Vilma wouldn't ask. Now it was put to her she couldn't avoid answering. She said: "There's a hitch, Vilma."

Vilma frowned. "A hitch? I don't get you."

"We've lost it."

"You've lost . . ." Vilma's expression was of mingled disbelief and astonishment. "When? How?"

Jill longed for Nina's support; but Nina had continued into the school with Lindy.

"I don't know when—and I don't know how."

"But you must know when you saw it last," Vilma said, with a touch of impatience.

Jill told her, reminding Vilma that she was in the common-room at the time, writing a letter.

"That's true," Vilma said. "*Trying* to write a letter, with Ruth and Denise on at me . . . Ruth!" She positively scowled. Then she said urgently: "Jill—your stuff was in a folder, wasn't it? Well, Ruth was looking through it. Only curiosity; wanted to take a sly squint at the sketch most likely to compete with our own. I told her off, too. I can't think she would. . . . No! But still—I'll check on it. And if Ruth went back to that cupboard and put your folder somewhere else she's going to be sorry. Very sorry indeed."

"I don't suspect Ruth," Jill said quickly. "But suppose

—just as an outside chance—she did that. Well it would only be a joke, of course. So don't take it too seriously."

"Ruth gets rather wild ideas," Vilma said. "I've thought more than once lately that it's high time some of them were knocked out of her. So if she's respons-ible. . . ." There were the familiar indications of mount-ing temper.

Jill hastened to say: "I don't suppose for a minute she is."

"Well—if she isn't, what are you going to do?"

"We've not decided yet," Jill told her.

"Look. I'll hold over taking our sketch to Miss Latimer. That'll give you a few more days. Have you said anything to her?"

Jill shook her head.

"I'll see you again as soon as I've had this out with Ruth. But if she knows nothing, I'm licked. I can't think who else."

"Neither can I?" Jill said. "And I don't honestly think Ruth knows anything about it."

"Then who? Your sketch didn't dissolve into thin air."

Jill sighed. "I'll probably end up believing we never wrote it."

She left Vilma and went up to the common-room. Nina was sitting there alone.

"Taking Lindy out was a smashing success," Jill said.

Nina stood up. Her face was troubled as she held out an envelope. Jill glanced at it and caught her breath.

"In—in the magazine box?"

"In the magazine box," Nina confirmed grimly.

She took out the slip of paper and read the message in the familiar block letters. THINGS SEEM TO BE GOING

WELL FOR JILL BUT HOW DOES SHE EXPLAIN THE MISSING SKETCH? SHE'LL BE VERY SILLY IF SHE GOES TO MISS LATIMER FOR HELP, BECAUSE MISS LATIMER ISN'T AS FRIENDLY AS JILL IMAGINES.

Jill felt a little wave of sickness. "This is just horrible!" she cried.

"Steady," Nina said quietly. "Don't get rattled. I'm sure that's exactly what the writer wants."

It made sense, Jill realised that. But it was one thing to realise one should keep calm; trying to do it was quite different. She certainly was badly rattled. "I'm wondering what this bit about Miss Latimer means," she said slowly.

Nina was certain it was intended to keep Jill from going to the form mistress about the missing script.

"I wasn't planning to!" Jill exclaimed when Nina explained this. "It's a nasty mess and it would worry her. We'd have to tell about the anonymous notes as well."

Nina nodded. She agreed with Jill. Miss Latimer had been very decent about their dash to town after Lindy. While it proved she was an understanding person, it also made them very anxious not to bother her again so soon.

Jill said reluctantly: "Of course, if things go on happening we may have to tell her in the end. But I hope it won't come to that."

"Oh, surely it won't!" Nina said. But secretly she wished she could feel much more confident.

It was during the next morning that something occured which was very important in their effort to track down the sender of the spiteful notes. It didn't seem at all significant at the time, though. Instead of going across to the science lab, that lesson was postponed and Miss Latimer took the fourth form for history.

The lesson passed uneventfully and not too slowly, because Miss Latimer had quite a talent for re-creating the past and presenting the characters as real people. Judy, never outstanding at concentrating on any subject, was inclined to grumble when they took their mid-morning break.

"If Miss Latimer would divide all those people into goods and bads I'd get a clearer idea," she said plaintively. "She makes them part good, part bad."

"Like real people," Jill said.

Judy edged nearer and lowered her voice. "Jill, I've been wanting to ask you—have you found your play yet?"

Jill shook her head and reminded Judy of the promise to say nothing. Judy vowed she hadn't breathed a word to a soul. She added: "But Jill, I think *somebody* knows something, because I couldn't help overhearing Vilma saying to Ruth about someone having taken something and had Ruth done it, and Ruth was terribly upstage and said she hadn't taken the folder and what's more she was very resentful about being suspected." Judy paused for breath. Then she managed to add: "It could've been the folder with your play in it."

"It's possible," Jill said. "But you'd better keep that to yourself, Judy. If Vilma hears . . ."

"You told me to let you know if I heard anything," Judy protested. "And I *am* being jolly careful—especially where Vilma's concerned. She gets mad so fast! Do you know, she once threatened to gag me!"

Jill grunted sympathetically, though to be honest she'd often had a rather similar idea about Judy.

"It's not fair, the way everybody picks on me," Judy

went on. "Not that I care. If the Fourth doesn't like to hear news it can go without."

Jill gave her a swift, suspicious glance. "And what's the latest tit-bit?" she asked.

Judy shook her head. "There isn't one. Perhaps it's after the excitement over Lindy." She looked about her and then hurried off, so quickly that Jill glanced round to discover the reason. Vilma Blake was coming towards her.

Vilma, nodding in Judy's direction, said: "That tongue been clattering again?"

"Nothing important," Jill said quickly.

"Rarely is. We ought to call her the yak-yak girl. If someone organised a non-stop talking competition we could win with Judy." Then, with a swift change to her more normal seriousness Vilma went on: "I've spoken to Ruth about your sketch. I'm sure she isn't involved."

"Thanks for asking her," Jill said.

Vilma frowned. "Afraid I wasn't tactful enough. She's taken it badly." There was a crinkly smile at one corner of her mouth. "Much more like that and the Vilma-for-captain movement's going to fade right out."

Jill felt rather awkward. Vilma was inclined to say things which caused embarrassment. Someone had suggested it appealed to her particular sense of humour.

It was impossible to ignore the remark, so Jill said: "You mustn't lose supporters on my account." And as Vilma looked at her with widening eyes, Jill continued: "Well, you *are* my rival, aren't you?" She grinned amiably.

Vilma chuckled. "Touché!" she said. "I admit I wanted to be captain, Jill. Now, I'm not so sure. I'm watching you carefully—but it's because I'm looking for the first grey hairs. They're supposed to come with worry."

"If so, my whole head will turn silver any minute," Jill said, and the break period ending at this moment they went back into the form room together. It was the first time this had happened and Jill felt that quite a number of girls noticed and were a little curious. She caught an almost resentful glance from Ruth.

Once again it was a lesson by Miss Latimer who, as soon as she'd taken her place, made a special announcement. Jill, listening with fascinated attention, could scarcely believe what she heard. During the morning the Head had received a surprise visit from Miss Garfield, who'd announced that she was going to grant the Hazelmere girls the same use of the woods they'd enjoyed in the past. Wire fences were being put up but there'd be gates at points nearest the school. The girls must recognise, though, that the whole of the enclosure was now a bird sanctuary and also understand that they must not enter when filming was taking place.

After a stunned surprise there was great enthusiasm over this news. Jill felt that many inquiring glances were being directed at Nina and herself. It wasn't hard to guess why, so she was prepared for the barrage of questions at the end of morning classes.

She raised her hands for silence and said: "I didn't know it was going to happen. I was with Nina and Lindy yesterday afternoon and Miss Garfield asked us to do some bird spotting for her. And we stayed for tea."

Denise insisted: "But you must have dropped hints about the freedom of the woods, surely?"

Jill smiled. "One doesn't drop hints to Miss Garfield. You'll get that right away if you ever meet her."

Muriel said: "I was sure from the start that there'd be no joy from Miss Garfield. How wrong can you get? But I still think Jill must have had a lot to do with the change of heart—helped by Nina, of course. Well—as this isn't a meeting I can't propose a vote of thanks. What's in a vote of thanks, anyway? It doesn't cost anything."

"Is that a suggestion the form should stand treat?" a girl named Clare asked. "If so, I second it."

"It—it would be a feast for us *all*, wouldn't it?" Judy asked anxiously. "If so, I third it!"

There was general laughter at this and so much teasing of the indignant Judy that the original suggestion was forgotten. Jill, relieved, turned to Nina and said: "Let's get out of here before anyone else gets a bright idea."

"I hear the gong," Nina said.

The animated under-current of excitement persisted throughout the meal. As they were all leaving the dining-room Mary Curtis of the Fifth stopped to have a word with Jill. "Is the latest Miss Garfield development a bit more of your work?" she asked.

Jill shook her head. "I was as surprised as anybody."

"Well, if they want to give you some of the credit, I'd say take it. You started better relationships with the dragon."

"Who really is no dragon," Nina said.

"I'll reserve judgment until I see her." Mary Curtis grinned. "I'm something of an expert on dragons. It comes of having them in my own family. We're rather proud of them. Hire 'em out." And with this amazing bit of information she hurried away.

Jill laughed. "I wonder what'll happen when Mary gets into the sixth and becomes a prefect."

"She'll never be a second Hilda Wighton—that's for sure," Nina said.

They made their way to the common-room, overtaking Lindy. In the corridor Ann Page was just turning away from the notice board. She hurried past them without the slightest sign of recognition.

"Is she afraid we'll stop her and try to talk to her?" Jill wondered.

"So far as I'm concerned she can get lost," Nina said.

"I certainly wouldn't worry about *her*," Lindy remarked.

She went on into the common-room, but Jill and Nina paused to read the new notice which Ann Page had evidently pinned up. It merely gave the official news of the permission for the girls to use the woods.

Nina said: "You know, in spite of what you've told them, most of the form are going to credit you with this —and probably other forms will, too."

"I don't want the credit," Jill argued. "Look—it'd be far more reasonable to say that Lindy was responsible. She was the one Miss Garfield took aside for a heart to heart. She spotted more birds than either of us. And she's been invited to tea."

"I don't think Lindy would like to have everyone congratulating her or making a fuss of her—not yet. By the way, she's very quiet to-day. She had a letter this morning and did she look solemn while she was reading it!"

Jill sighed. "Oh, I hope it wasn't bad news. She didn't say anything about it?"

"Not a word."

During the afternoon Jill looked across at Lindy several times. The girl didn't look particularly upset;

but she did seem to have even more on her mind than the actual lessons, indeed sometimes Jill was certain she was thinking of entirely different things.

When lessons were over and the girls were leaving the form room, Ruth pushed her way across and came to Jill's side.

"Did you tell Vilma you thought I'd pinched your rotten old sketch?" Ruth demanded.

Jill was surprised by the sudden attack; but she wasn't at all slow with her reply. "I didn't and I don't."

Ruth appeared disconcerted. "You mean—it was her idea?"

Anxious to prevent any trouble Jill said as soothingly as she could: "It was only that Vilma remembered you'd had it out. . . ."

Ruth flushed. "I shouldn't have done that. I'm sorry. It was just nosiness."

"No need to apologise. If you wanted to see it you could have done."

"Ought to have asked. The way Vilma pitched into me! I hadn't realised what I was . . ." Ruth hesitated, looked round as if making sure that they were alone. Then she said: "Look, Jill. When there was an election for form captain I backed Vilma. You won—but I've kept it up, thinking something might happen to cause another election. . . ." She stopped, a bit confused.

"If I made a mess of things and there was a pretty strong demand for me to resign?" Jill suggested.

"It sounds bad put that way," Ruth confessed.

Jill smiled. "It's only that you were very loyal to your pal."

"And she's not worth it, anyway. Her temper! She storms at everybody, including her best friends," grumbled Ruth.

"You're exaggerating," Jill said. "She flares up, but she doesn't exactly storm."

"I've had more than enough. I'm not going to be accused of things I haven't done."

"Not to worry," Jill insisted. "Everybody'd satisfied you didn't, so forget it. Just forget it."

"I'm not going to forget the way Vilma spoke to me," Ruth said stubbornly.

"She didn't mean it, and she'll apologise."

They'd been walking slowly towards the common-room. At the last minute Ruth said impulsively: "Talking of apologies . . . I'm sorry, Jill. As a captain you're the best."

"Thank you!" Jill gasped, taken completely by surprise.

Ruth darted into the common-room and Jill went on towards the stairs but was checked by Nina, who came running to her and seized her arm so tightly that it positively hurt.

"Ow! What's this in aid of?" Jill demanded. "I want my arm!"

Nina released her with a quick apology. "Sorry. Jill, I've made a discovery. Come along to the library right away."

Jill blinked. "A discovery?"

"Our spiteful anonymous enemy's slipped up at last. I think we can track her down now!"

CHAPTER SIXTEEN

SHOW-DOWN

"I HOPE you really have got something to tell me," Jill panted when they reached the library. Nina had caught her by the arm again and positively hustled her all the way.

"I didn't want anyone to see us going into a huddle," Nina explained. "Another thing, you'd been so long I was getting impatient."

Jill smiled. "You don't say!"

Nina thrust a slip of paper at her. "Just look at this!"

It was yet another of the unsigned notes. Jill recognised the block letters immediately. In spite of Nina's encouraging words Jill experienced the same slight feeling of sickness as she started to read. This was a longer one than the others. It read: WHEN JILL WAS GOING ACROSS TO THE LAB FOR SCIENCE, DID SHE SEE MISS GARFIELD ARRIVE? YOU BET—AND SHE RAN ACROSS TO LICK HER SHOES. JUST HOW LOW CAN YOU GET WHEN YOU'RE ON THE CADGE?

"It's as beastly as the rest!" Jill exclaimed. Her cheeks had gone hot.

"Steady on!" Nina said. "It's a lot of bosh. But it tells us plenty."

Jill shook her head. She was still too upset by the unpleasant accusation to think clearly.

"Wake up!" Nina urged. "Take another look and think—think hard. What's true?"

Jill read it again and said: "Miss Garfield came to see

the Head this morning, of course. We all know that's true." Then she realised where the writer had made a mistake. "Of course! We didn't go across to the lab."

"Exactly," Nina said. "And whoever wrote this wasn't aware the lessons had been changed. So . . ."

"Of course!" Jill clapped her hands together, her eyes shining. "Aren't I dim! So the writer can't be one of our form!"

This was a tremendous relief to Jill, who felt she could at last be free of the horrible suspicion that a member of the Fourth was vindictive towards her. "I'm so happy about it I'm not going to worry even if there are more messages," she exclaimed.

"It's got to be stopped, Jill," Nina said soberly.

Jill looked at her thoughtfully and then nodded. If the campaign against herself failed, somebody else might become the victim. There was no knowing. She said: "I suppose you're right. But we still have to find out *who*." She waved the note. "This only clears the fourth form."

"You're wrong. It does more than that," Nina insisted. To begin with, the writer was someone who knew at what time Miss Garfield called on the Head but wasn't aware of the changed time-table for the fourth form.

Jill said: "Of course, she could be guessing at the time Miss Garfield came."

"Why—when she was in a position to *know*?" Nina demanded.

Jill stared at her. "What are you saying?"

"They keep all the lessons time-tables over in the office," Nina said. "And they'd see anyone who called on the Head. And there's one person who works over there, who certainly isn't friendly."

"Ann Page!" Jill gasped. Then she shook her head.

"No, Nina, listen! You're going too fast. This can't be right. I don't know her—she doesn't know me. There just isn't any reason. And there has to be some sort of reason—even a crazy one—for these notes."

Nina was prepared to grant that she hadn't a clue as to any motive.

Jill shook her head. "And there isn't any proof, either," she said. "She had the chance to do it—but no motive. It's pretty weak."

"When we went after Lindy we could have been seen from the offices as we rushed for the gates," Nina said. "I had an awful feeling the Head was watching us. But suppose Ann Page saw us and told Hilda Wighton? After all, she could make it seem she had the best interests of the school at heart."

"That's true enough," Jill admitted. But it still, to her mind, didn't make a convincing case. "It's like the rest," she said. "Ann Page *could*, but there's no reason why she *should*. That makes sense, doesn't it?"

Nina had to agree that it did, but she wasn't going to give up. "I'm going on from here," she said. "Something tells me I'm on the right track."

"Not just because Ann Page has been snubbing us?"

"It's a hunch," Nina declared. "This builds up, Jill. The culprit isn't a fourth form girl, yet she knows quite a bit of what goes on in the form. Ann Page is friendly with Judy and Judy's the biggest careless talker in the school."

Jill pointed out that Judy was never really disloyal.

"Of course not," Nina agreed. "But Judy goes to see Ann Page. Judy jabbers and Ann Page listens. She hears a lot of rubbish—but she also hears useful bits."

This, Jill accepted. "If only we could question Judy," she said thoughtfully. "I'm afraid it wouldn't be safe, though. We warned her to keep quiet about the missing folder and somehow she managed it—but this would be riskier."

Nina shared this view. Assuming their theory was correct Judy might easily put Ann Page on her guard. And if they were wrong they might find themselves in real trouble.

"It'd be slander, for sure," Nina said gloomily. She paced to one of the windows and back again. "Very well. We can't question Judy. And there's no one else. . . ." She strode to the window and stared out. Suddenly she swung round. "There is! At least, there may be."

"Who?"

"Do you remember Lindy saying something about Ann Page?"

Jill thought for a moment. "Yes. When Ann Page cut us, by the notice board. But I don't think Lindy knows her."

"You forget. Lindy's hung around coffee bars in town. You know what she was like before she snapped out of it. She could well have bumped into Ann Page somewhere."

Jill was far from convinced but agreed that it might be worth asking Lindy. For one reason and another, there was no opportunity to do this until after bedtime. Then Lindy came with Nina to Jill's bedside. She said, her manner a little shy: "One thing I wanted to mention, Jill."

"Go ahead," Jill encouraged.

"The concert. It seems a long time ago—but you did ask me if I'd do a vocal spot."

"You're the Fourth's best singer and I wanted to nab you for our effort. Nina's and mine, I mean. Our first idea was to put up a sort of review, with you doing two vocals."

Lindy said earnestly: "I just can't say how sorry I am. Not only about refusing, but the way I refused. Well—if you still want me . . ."

Jill and Nina exchanged swift glances. "We'd be jolly glad to have you. But there's a big problem. Nina and I switched to writing a sketch, with just one song parody that Nina could manage to sing if she had to. And we were all ready to put it up for approval, when . . . but surely you've heard about it?"

Lindy shook her head, looking puzzled.

"I'd have thought the story must have leaked by now," Jill said.

Lindy gave a faint smile. "Most of the girls are still tongue-tied when I'm around. They mean to be kind, of course; but I wish they'd just forget."

"How *are* things going?" asked Nina.

"The Head said she'd write to my mother. She may have done so, but I've had a letter that was written a week ago. Mother's a bit careless with non-business correspondence. She says she's frightfully sorry but she'll be in America when the next hols come along, and she's telling me in good time because of making arrangements. Do I want to go and stay with my aunt, or would I rather stay at home with Mrs. Tate to look after me." She pulled a long face. "Not hilarious either way."

"How utterly rotten!" Nina exclaimed. "Have you told the Head?"

"Not exactly. I showed Miss Latimer the letter. She didn't say much—just said she was glad I showed her and she'd have a word with the Head."

"Something must be arranged," Jill said. "Don't worry more than you can help." She looked anxiously at Lindy.

"I'm not going to get in a state," Lindy promised.

"Being able to talk about it makes quite a difference. But what's the story I should have heard?"

"Oh, that!" Jill had been completely side-tracked. As briefly as possible she told Lindy all that had happened.

"But this is dreadful!" Lindy whispered. She was sitting on the edge of the bed and she moved so that she could lean towards Nina. "Who on earth could be so absolutely mean to Jill? She's proving the best captain the Fourth's ever had."

This tribute surprised both Jill and Nina, for everyone knew that Lindy had said there'd never be anyone as good as Pam Ralston.

"Do I tell her?" Nina asked, after a slight pause.

"I should think so. After all, she's been involved in it. When Hilda Wighton nabbed us it could have been darn serious for Lindy. So she's a right to know."

"It sounds terrifically mysterious," said Lindy.

Nina told her of their suspicions. Lindy listened in complete silence. When Nina had finished Jill said: "But there's no real proof, Lindy. In fact, accusing Ann Page just doesn't make sense, does it?"

Lindy didn't reply. She sat for a minute or so, head lowered. Then she jumped up. "Jill—I'm not sure. There may be an answer; but I've got to think about it."

"You mean you know something about Ann Page?" Nina demanded.

Lindy was obviously very worried. "Please don't ask any questions—not now." She turned and hurried across to her bed.

"What d'you make of that?" Nina whispered.

Jill shook her head. "I don't. I'm just not with it." She stifled a yawn. "Let's leave it till to-morrow. Right

now I don't feel the best captain the Fourth's ever had.
I only feel the tiredest."

The next morning Lindy seemed to be trying to avoid
Jill and Nina. She had a preoccupied expression which
suggested she was wrestling with some sort of problem.

Nina whispered to Jill: "I'm just dying to know; but
I don't think we should hurry her, do you?"

"Leave her to work it out her own way," Jill agreed.

In the afternoon, lessons finished early because of tennis
practice. After changing, Jill and Nina hurried downstairs, determined to make up for the time lost when they
had dashed in to town after Lindy.

"We'll be so much off form that we'll have Vilma
dropping us from the team," Jill said.

"I wish she'd be shockingly off form herself, some
time," Nina commented. "It'd be good for her—and for
us; but it never seems to happen." Her wish was almost
granted, though, for when she played a set against Vilma
it went to fourteen-twelve before Nina was defeated.

"Phew! She's like lightning!" Vilma gasped as she
flopped on to a chair which Jill had just vacated. "I
don't know about her endurance; but if that held,
she'd beat me in a proper three-set match on to-day's
form."

Jill was glad to hear the tribute. She said cautiously:
"We're going to need her!"

Vilma looked up at her. "You played Denise. How
did it go?"

"I won," Jill said.

"Go on. Tell me more."

"She was a bit slow getting started," Jill said.

"But the result?" Vilma pressed.

"If you must know—it was six-one."

Vilma thumped her racket on the grass. "She ought to have done better than that!" she exclaimed.

"I think there's some improvement in her play," Jill said, anxious to prevent a storm breaking over the unfortunate Denise.

"Six-one! It sounds like it! And the time I spent coaching her when we were last on court!"

"Everyone gets a bit off form sometimes," Jill urged. "After all, you shouldn't have had so much trouble in coping with Nina."

"It's not the same," Vilma declared. "You could say Nina's the school's best dancer. Agreed?"

"I think so, yes."

"Of course she is!" Vilma was a bit snappish. "And when we have athletics, who wins the hundred yards every time? As for tennis—Nina's got so much speed and her footwork's so good she makes every opponent look slow and lumbering. And that includes me." Vilma jumped up and went striding towards Denise.

Nina joined Jill. "That's enough, isn't it? Time's up and I'm tired of dashing around."

Jill nodded. "Might as well go back. I see Miss Frant's on her way."

"She was playing Lindy. Did you notice?"

Jill hadn't realised this. She wondered if it had been sheerly by chance or whether Miss Frant was carrying out the Head's wishes. It could well have been part of a policy to keep Lindy interested in as much as possible.

Lindy had already left the courts, but Jill and Nina overtook her.

"How did the tennis go?" Jill asked.

Lindy shook her head. "I wasn't good. Vilma's right to have dropped me. I couldn't put up any sort of a show.

My backhand was always suspect." She smiled wryly. "Not so any longer. It's shown itself as plain dreadful."

"You've neglected it," said Nina. "All it needs is some practice."

They walked on in silence. Jill was wondering how to bring up the subject they'd discussed on the previous night. They were beginning to get on well with Lindy, but she was still rather unpredictable.

While Jill was thinking, Lindy suddenly said: "I suppose you want from me all I can give about Ann Page."

"Might help," said Jill.

"Perhaps it'd put an end to a situation that's getting unbearable," Nina urged. "What's going to happen next? And what will the next nasty spiteful note say? Don't you see how awful it is, Lindy?"

"Are you sure Ann Page is guilty?" Lindy challenged.

Jill hesitated. It was one thing to have very strong suspicions; but to be absolutely certain. . . . She sighed. "I don't know. She seems the most likely suspect."

Nina cried: "Of course we're not sure. But it looks very much that way. Just listen." She went through all the arguments for Ann Page being the one who had opportunity each time. "Even," she finished, "to being wonderfully free to drop the notes in the mag box. She's always wandering round the notice boards, pinning things up or taking them down."

"You could be right," Lindy said.

"If you know something—tell us," Nina persisted.

"It's not quite so simple," Lindy said. "Tell you what —let's go and see her. If you'll bring the last message, Nina. Our best time will be in about twenty minutes, immediately after tea."

"Okay," Jill said. The Head usually had her tea a little later and the bursar nearly always joined her. Matron,

too, was often there. This should leave Ann Page undis-
turbed for a time.

"So we change fast and grab a quick cuppa," Nina
said.

"Then try to slip away without the rest of the form
wondering what we're up to," Jill finished for her.

As it happened, they were able to do this without
difficulty. The atmosphere in the common room was
not so friendly as usual. Ruth had suddenly taken Vilma
to task for something she said. Denise eagerly supported
Ruth. It was a new experience for Vilma to be challenged by members of her own circle and most of the
other girls were fascinated onlookers.

Safely away, Jill said: "Ruth's still sore about being
accused of pinching our play. And I suppose Vilma
went for Denise over her weak tennis."

"Vilma's going to have to learn to be much more
patient," Nina commented. She turned to Lindy. "This
last note to the magazine. Do you want to have it? Or
do I keep it?"

"You keep it," Lindy said. "Nina—I think you should
speak first. Give it to Ann Page and tell her it isn't
suitable for the fourth form mag."

Nina stared. "Gosh!"

"Trust me," Lindy urged. "I think I know the best
way to handle this."

"You know more than we do, then," Jill said. "A
heck of a lot more. I'm groping."

"Ever heard of Ann Page? Before she turned up here,
I mean."

"No."

"Your home's not awfully far away."

"The other side town. About ten miles. What's that
to do with all this?"

Ignoring the question, Lindy asked: "Ever heard of Stan Page?"

"Never." Jill shook her head. "And this is getting me all confused."

"I'm afraid it'll be very clear—if Ann Page is guilty," Lindy said.

When they reached the door to the offices Lindy turned quickly to Jill. "I'm bothered," she confessed. "Perhaps I ought to have told you things—but if you knew in advance I'm not sure it'd work out right."

She hurried inside. Jill and Nina exchanged puzzled glances and followed. Ann Page was alone and apparently she was just finishing a tea break. A tray was pushed to the end of her desk and she was reading a glossy magazine. She looked up sharply and then scowled. Watching her closely, though, Jill thought she was a bit uneasy.

"What do you kids want?" Ann Page spoke sharply.

Lindy nudged Nina, who stepped forward and said: "Miss Page, I'm sorry, but this just isn't suitable for the fourth form magazine."

Nina pushed the slip of paper towards Ann Page and stepped back. Jill, giving all her attention, heard Ann Page catch her breath. There was a moment of silence and then the typist jumped up and faced them.

"Get out! All of you! Get out of here! I won't have you barging in here and talking nonsense!"

It was too violent and Jill felt certain it must be a cover for guilt. She said quietly: "Why these attacks on me, Miss Page?"

For the first time Lindy spoke. "Do I tell her about Stan, or do you?"

Ann Page turned very pale. She turned on Lindy. "How do you know?" she demanded.

"I've heard things," Lindy said.

"Will someone tell us just what all this is about?" Nina asked.

There was a slight pause. Then Ann Page moved close to Jill, her eyes narrowed, one finger pointing accusingly. "Okay! I did it. I wanted you to be miserably unhappy."

Jill stared at her blankly. "Unhappy! But why?"

"Don't you know about my brother? Stan?"

Jill shook her head.

"You should," Ann Page snapped. "Your father killed him."

"Killed him? What absolute nonsense!" Jill cried.

"Driving too fast one night. Round Saxon Cross corner. Stan was on his motor-bike and your father was in his car. Stan didn't have a chance." Ann Page was looking so fierce that Jill backed away slightly.

Lindy said: "Wait a minute. There was an inquest. If Jill's father was to blame it would've come out then."

Ann Page pointed at Jill. "With her father a doctor— and the coroner a doctor? They stuck together. So Stan was to blame—he was the one who couldn't speak for himself, you see."

"This is the first I've heard of it," Jill protested. "I know my father doesn't talk much about what's happened, but surely I'd have known. When was it?"

"You don't know!" Ann Page exclaimed scornfully.

Lindy said: "It was last summer, Jill. During the hols. Last week in July."

"I wasn't here. I went to France, to stay with Doctor Benoit and his family near Rheims. Their daughter Juliette's about my age. But that's not important." She looked straight at Ann Page. "I'm very sorry to hear about your brother. I *didn't* know of it, but I'm sure it wasn't my father's fault."

"Why take it out on Jill anyway?" Nina demanded.

"I lost a lot when I lost my brother," the typist said. "And when I came here and found she was at the school —well, I decided to make her suffer a bit. No way of getting my own back on her father."

"It doesn't make sense!" Nina snapped. "Jill didn't have anything to do with your brother's death."

"Neither did I. I suffered, though. So why shouldn't she?"

"Still doesn't make sense," Nina said contemptuously.

"To me it does!" Ann Page cried.

Lindy moved nearer. "There's something you don't know about that accident, Miss Page," she said quietly.

Ann Page swung round to face her. "What don't I know?"

"I've heard a lot about it," Lindy said. "I started this term feeling pretty fed up with school and I've been into town every possible chance I had of getting there. Yes—and I've sneaked back late. I've met older girls at one or two of the coffee bars. There's one who used to go around with a boy named Harry Wade."

"Harry Wade!" Ann Page looked startled.

"This girl—her name's Gladys—told me quite a lot about Harry. How he used to race about on his motor-bike. Doing a ton, he called it."

"Fine crowd you've been mixing with. I don't know this Gladys, but I do know what Harry Wade's like. I warned Stan. . . ." Ann Page stopped, biting her lip.

Lindy said: "Gladys told me that Harry Wade did the disappearing act the day after your brother was killed. He didn't want it to come out that he'd had a stupid wager with Stan. Out to Saxon Cross, grab an empty Saxon Farm milk bottle from outside one of the houses and be back in under thirty minutes."

"No! I don't believe it! Stan promised. . . ."

"It meant doing a ton for some of the way," Lindy
went on. "Harry Wade admitted to Gladys that he saw
Stan taking that bend so fast he couldn't get round it.
Then there was a horrible scream of brakes and a crash.
Harry simply pulled up as hard as he dared and turned
back. Looked after himself. He told Gladys you have
to be smart in this world."

Ann Page didn't say a word this time. Her head was
lowered and she went very slowly to her desk. She sat
down and covered her face with her hands.

Jill hesitated, angry at the meanness and the stupid
spite of the typist's attacks on her, longing to say exactly
what she thought and in that way give vent to her own
pent up feelings; but at the same time understanding a
little of the suffering and brooding that had caused the
girl to have such a distorted outlook. She must have
been through an awful lot, Jill decided, her own wrath
already beginning to evaporate, especially as there'd be
no more trouble from this source.

She touched Nina's arm and whispered: "Best to leave
her alone." She signed to Lindy and they all moved
quietly towards the door.

Suddenly Ann Page called: "Come back! Please!"
She looked hard at Lindy. "Is that true—all you've
told me?"

"Exactly what Gladys said to me," Lindy confirmed.

"It's easy to believe that about Harry Wade. He was
poison. There's no other word for it. But Stan promised
he'd break with Harry; said he'd have nothing to do with
him. Stan was always a bit weak—but I was so sure,
this time!"

Jill pushed Nina and Lindy through the open doorway
and would have followed them but for a choking sob

from Ann Page. Jill turned back. "I'm sorry about your brother," she said. "But don't brood any more. Try to forget it."

Ann Page didn't answer. Her shoulders were shaking and Jill went across to her. "You'll feel better when you get over the shock and . . ." she started to say.

"I shan't. I've been such a—such a . . . Look what I've done to you! I'll have to go and tell Miss Manley. I'll confess. . . ."

"There's only one thing you need do," Jill said. "If you took the folder containing our sketch, you can return it." It took quite an effort to keep back the few biting words she would have liked to add when a momentary vision of the distress she and Nina had experienced over the sketch flashed into her mind.

Ann Page opened a drawer, took out the folder and gave it to Jill.

"How did you know where we'd left it?"

"Judy was in here, chattering, and she said something about a girl named Ruth taking a peep at it and some sort of a row developing. It gave me the idea. I waited until I knew the coast would be clear and went across into your common-room."

Jill tucked the folder under her arm. "Nobody else need know about any of this," she said.

"Hilda Wighton knows I sneaked on you when you slipped off in to town with Nina. . . ."

"Well, that was something you really should have reported," Jill said. "But for the rest . . ."

"You mean you'll forgive me?" Ann Page looked bewildered.

"Sure. You've brooded and brooded and got things all mixed up and made yourself sour. You'll get yourself sorted out again now, I reckon."

Ann Page smiled tearfully. "I'll have a bash, as you'd say. Honestly, Jill, I won't ever do anything like it again."

CHAPTER SEVENTEEN

TEA WITH MISS GEE

ABOUT a fortnight after the showdown with Ann Page and the end of the miserable business of the anonymous notes, Jill and Nina were invited to tea with Miss Garfield.

"Commanded would be more like it," Jill murmured, remembering the very short letter written with an extremely broad nib. She was walking through the wood with Nina and they were almost in sight of the house.

"I wonder why she didn't invite Lindy as well," Nina said. "At least, I suppose she hasn't. I didn't like to ask Lindy, for fear of making her feel she's missing something."

"I've got a feeling you're way off the beam, pal. I think she comes and goes as she likes and I bet she's already here. Haven't you noticed that she seems to head this way an awful lot lately and doesn't need us any more? It's strange how well they get along together."

"You may well be right. I hope so," Nina said. "I think Miss Garfield's just the sort of person Lindy needed in order to get her ideas sorted out. And Lindy liked her on sight. Remember?"

"Certainly *something*'s made Lindy very much happier. I'm awfully glad."

"So'm I."

As the two girls came out from the wood and started to cross the lawn Nina pointed in the direction of a greenhouse which had been converted into an aviary. "There's Lindy! How right you were!"

Miss Garfield appeared. "Hurry up, you two. I begin to want my tea and there's a job to do first."

Nina said under her breath: "Now what are we going to be let in for? I admire this woman a lot—but she is a bit of a menace."

It quickly transpired that the job was for Jill to perform. One of the budgerigars needed attention.

"Lindy doesn't know how to do it and I'd be too clumsy —so you cut this claw. You know how?"

Jill nodded. "Oh, yes. I've often done it, Miss Garfield."

The patient had been isolated in a small cage. Jill extricated it deftly, with a minimum of fluttering. She held the bird with just the right firmness so that it seemed it had confidence in her. The operation was swiftly over and the bird was released, flying happily across the aviary to join its companions.

Miss Garfield, who'd remained quite silent for once, had stood near, watching intently. She didn't move until Jill had finished; then she stepped forward and said: "The quicker you grow up, leave school, and qualify, the better. There's going to be plenty of work for you here. I'll be glad to be rid of old Barton."

Jill had heard of a veterinary surgeon of this name. She said: "I've heard he's very good, Miss Garfield."

"I'm not criticising his work. He's all right. Fumbles a bit, though. You'll be better—you've got the magic touch. But the truth is, he doesn't like me. He's very set in his ways and he doesn't think women should answer back. Nerve!"

Lindy, standing close to her, laughed. "Or is it that he answers *you* back?" she teased.

"Not nearly so much as you do," Miss Garfield said. "Of course, I've grown out of it now; but I used to be a bit of a terror for speaking my mind and having the last word. So I can't condemn it in others. I'll go and make that Gertrude hurry with the tea." She turned round and bustled back into the house, leaving the girls together.

"Used to be," Jill whispered. "Did I hear her say she used to be?"

Nina, gurgling with amusement, said: "Yes. She's grown out of it now. You heard the lady."

Jill spread her hands in a gesture of helplessness. "I give up." She looked at Lindy. "You seem to get along wonderfully. Doesn't she bully you?"

Lindy shook her head. "Not really. And I'm so happy about being able to come here when I'm free. I say— I've had a terrific surprise to-day—wonderful news! Miss Garfield told me when I arrived."

"What?" Jill demanded.

"Don't keep woffling around. Give," Nina urged. She was equally curious.

"Well, it seems Miss Gee suggested it to the Head when she saw her—and the Head approved and wrote to Mother—and—well—I'm going to spend the hols with Miss Gee."

"That's magnificent!" Jill exclaimed.

"It'll certainly never be dull," Nina said, a twinkle in her eyes.

"It's going to be so wonderful just not being ignored," Lindy said, and almost immediately went on: "Miss Gee says we must get away somewhere; but I don't think it can be managed. The horses will be coming here then, you see, and that'll mean a lot of work. Some of them will have to be ridden to make sure they get a little exercise and Miss Gee doesn't ride much."

"Should suit you," Jill said.

"I know. I'm mad on horses. And there are two that Miss Gee's rescued from one of those tatty riding schools that are so bad. They've been overworked but they mustn't be left doing nothing, and Miss Gee says I can regard one as mine. What d'you think of that?"

"Super!" Nina exclaimed. "Absolutely super!" She stepped very close to Lindy and lowered her voice. "Why do you call her Miss Gee? I'm intrigued."

"Well, she says she's sort of adopted me as a niece, but I mustn't call her aunt because she was christened Geraldine and she's sure Aunt Geraldine's an impossible name for her."

Jill and Nina laughed, and Jill observed that one really did have to strain the imagination to see Miss Garfield as an Aunt Geraldine.

Further talk was cut short by Miss Garfield calling from the house: "I don't know about you girls, but I'm dying of hunger and thirst. Come on and have tea."

"She's a shocker!" Lindy exclaimed, giggling. "Last Sunday I tried to start her on a diet to get down a bit of her weight. It's one a doctor had prepared for her. But I had to give up. She hides biscuits all over the place!"

And at tea Miss Garfield lived up to her reputation by examining a cake closely and saying: "I suppose this thin slice was cut for me. I'll show Gertrude!" Half the cake had been left uncut and Miss Garfield proceeded to carve an enormous wedge for herself. "This is better," she added. But Jill thought she looked rather apprehensively at Lindy.

Lindy said: "When I start my holidays you'll have to try that diet, Miss Gee. I'll be here to help."

"Help! You call that help!" Miss Garfield shouted indignantly.

Lindy smiled at her. She was at the parrot's cage, which she'd opened, and she was offering Diogenes an almond from the top of the cake. The parrot took it and then lowered his head to be scratched.

"If I did that the ungrateful wretch would bite me," Miss Garfield complained.

Still holding the nut in one claw the parrot turned his head to Miss Garfield and shrieked: "Belt up!"

"He'd be a riot if we could use him at the concert!" Jill cried.

"Oh, yes—how's that going?" Miss Garfield asked.

Jill explained that the sketch she and Nina had written had been approved. So had one by Vilma Blake. This had given great satisfaction to the entire form.

"I hope they're good," Miss Garfield said. "I'll be coming to it, you know. Have you put me down for a ticket?"

"I will," Jill promised.

"I want a free one," Miss Garfield announced.

Jill smiled. "Then you shall have a free one, Miss Garfield, I promise." She made a swift mental decision that if necessary she'd pay for it herself.

"The concert's for the new sports pavilion, isn't it?" Miss Garfield asked thoughtfully.

"Yes. We're hoping great things from it," Jill replied.

"Tell your headmistress I'll send her a cheque for fifty pounds," Miss Garfield announced. "But I get a free ticket, mind."

Fifty pounds! Jill, like the other girls, was speechless for a moment. And this gave Diogenes his chance. Before Jill could start to stammer her thanks he announced at the top of his quite powerful voice: "She's off her rocker!"